THE SECRET
WISH

THE SECRET WISH

WISH

•

Annette Mahon

AVALON BOOKS
NEW YORK

Published by Thomas Bouregy & Co., Inc.
160 Madison Avenue, New York, NY 10016

Library of Congress Cataloging-in-Publication Data

Mahon, Annette.
    The secret wish / Annette Mahon.
        p. cm.
    ISBN 0-8034-9754-7 (acid-free paper)
    I. Title.

    PS3563.A3595S443 2006
    813'.54—dc22

                            2005025390

PRINTED IN THE UNITED STATES OF AMERICA
ON ACID-FREE PAPER
BY HADDON CRAFTSMEN, BLOOMSBURG, PENNSYLVANIA

This book is dedicated to all of my faithful readers,
and especially to Georgia, my biggest fan.
To hear that my stories brought you a few hours
of pleasure is the reason I do this.

Chapter One

Abby Mana'olana'alohi Andrews frowned as she stared at the faded pink walls. It looked like a hundred bottles of stomach medicine had exploded in the long, narrow room.

Beside her, Aunty Liliuokalani frowned right back. "Don't look like that. This place is just what you need. A little paint and it will be perfect."

"Paint would help. . . ." Abby found her gaze drawn to the wide windows that lined the front of the room. "It is nice and bright."

Her godmother looked out the windows too. "Great view."

Abby laughed. It felt good to laugh. It broke through the doubts that had stressed her since she'd made the decision to move back to Malino.

"What view? The Dairy Queen?"

Indeed, the old house that had been Patty's Beauty Salon sat just across the road from Malino's popular hangout spot, making it the perfect place to catch the eye of the young girls in town—the clientele she most hoped to attract. While most of the Dairy Queen building couldn't be seen from the front windows, the tables grouped along one side held center stage in the wide "picture window." Abby didn't know if anyone outside Malino actually called the wide windows by that name any more—she'd never heard it in California—but people in Malino definitely did. She had to laugh at her "great view," even as she admitted that Aunty Lili had a point. What could be better for a hair salon than the opportunity for its clients to observe who was spending time with whom at the local hangout?

Aunty Lili dismissed Abby's laughter with a quick wave of her hand. "A little work, and this place will be fine," she said, echoing her earlier statement. "I got you someone to help fix it up. He should be here any time now. You remember Kevin Palea?"

"Remember him? I had the most awful crush on him back in second grade."

A deep masculine voice sounded behind them, laughter in its words.

"Oh, yeah? A big crush, huh?"

Startled by the new arrival, embarrassed that she

hadn't even heard him approach, Abby found herself blushing. At twenty-three, she'd thought herself long past blushing, but perhaps it was part of the atmosphere of Malino. The sweet, small-town flavor and the *'ohana* that flowed through the townspeople— that special Hawaiian bond of family that encompassed not only blood relations but shirt-tail relatives, neighbors and close friends—was what she sought to recapture.

Abby turned to confront the new addition to their little group. She might not have seen him since she was twelve years old, but she knew it was Kevin Palea—all grown up, and with the promise she must have seen back in second grade realized. If she hadn't sworn off men entirely, she would be interested. Very interested.

Kevin was tall, broad, and definitely a man who would attract a second or even a third look. Toned muscle defined the arms below his T-shirt sleeves and the legs beneath the baggy shorts.

But Kevin Palea wasn't just a buff body. He had bright eyes that sparkled with amusement at what he'd overheard, eyes that suggested a keen intelligence. He also had a wealth of rich brown hair, thick and healthy despite evidence of sun exposure; golden highlights gleamed in the sunlight that poured through the wide front windows. In California, clients paid big bucks to achieve that look, but Abby was sure that on Kevin it was the real thing.

Her professional eye judged the thick thatch, noting a lack of the dryness that could be a problem for islanders who spent a lot of time in the sun and sea. He wore his hair longer than she would recommend, and it badly needed shaping. But it had a natural wave that made the strands curl attractively around his ears and his nape—a look that probably drove the women wild.

But she'd had her fill of men for the time being. She was going to become an independent business-woman and develop lots of platonic friendships instead of one romantic relationship. Therefore, to begin what she thought of as their re-acquaintance, she refused to acknowledge her attraction.

"Kevin, I presume?" She put her hand forward, all business.

He nodded, equally serious as he shook her hand. "In the flesh."

Abby was impressed by his firm handshake. He didn't squeeze her hand too hard to show off his strength, or pretend to kiss it in some sort of roman-tic parody. His hand was large and rough, but gentle as well. A man who worked with his hands and knew his own strength.

But what impressed her most of all were his eyes. They smiled down at her—he was at least six inches taller than her five feet five—and sparkled with life. And the color! His eyes—despite his dark hair and obvious Polynesian heritage—were a clear, Pacific blue. He also had the longest eyelashes she'd ever seen on either a man or a woman—long, brown, and curling. If she'd ever wondered what the seven-year-old Abby had seen in the older Kevin, the answer was right before her eyes.

Aunty Lili greeted Kevin with a hug. "I was just telling Abby how you're going to help her out."

Shaking herself out of her enchantment with his appearance, Abby brought herself back to the business at hand.

"Ah, I don't have a lot of money available for fixing this place up," she began.

"No worry," Aunty Lili cut in, using a favorite pidgin phrase. "You forget, you're back in the islands now. This is *'ohana*. We all help one another."

'Ohana? This was what Abby had hoped to find by returning to Malino, of course. But she didn't want to misunderstand, so she turned toward Kevin. *'Ohana* meant family, though it could include a lot more than blood relatives. In this case she wanted to be sure. She hoped she wasn't rhapsodizing over a cousin's good looks. Yuck!

"Family? Are we related?"

"Well," he said, with a wide grin, "Aunty Lili is my godmother."

"And he's a good godson," Aunty Lili enthused. "He comes and helps me all the time. He's a good boy," she repeated, reaching up to ruffle his hair. Aunty Lili was a tall woman, but she still had to reach up to perform what appeared to be a well-practiced act.

Abby almost giggled at the look that crossed Kevin's face. But he bore it with good grace, even putting his arm around Aunty Lili's shoulders and giving her an affectionate squeeze.

"Aunty Lili really is my aunt," Abby said. "She's my mother's aunt. And she's my godmother too."

"When you live as long as me, you get lots of godchildren. I have twenty-two," she said proudly. Then a sadness swept through her eyes as she looked from one to the other. "I never had children of my own, but I have my nieces and nephews and all my godchildren. You two, you're still here, but most of them have moved away."

Abby felt lucky to be included as someone who was "still here," but she did feel a momentary guilt over the years she'd spent in California. Of course, she'd been too young to protest when her parents took her there, but there was no accounting for guilt.

Aunty Lili was still speaking about her godchildren. "They go to Honolulu or the mainland, looking for jobs. Some send Christmas cards to keep in touch. Some send cards for other holidays. But you . . ." She put an arm around each of the young people and squeezed. "You are two of the best. You are here. And you care for your old godmother."

Abby turned into Aunty Lili's arms and gave her a

hug. The old woman sounded dangerously close to tears, and soon Abby would be crying too.

Although Aunty was a tall, well-built woman, her bones felt thin and fragile beneath Abby's touch. And although the day was already warm, her skin felt quite cool. Abby couldn't help but notice the thickness and warmth of Kevin's arm in comparison. With Aunty Lili still hugging them both, he remained close and Abby found her arm pressed solidly against him. It was not an unpleasant sensation; in fact, it felt quite the opposite. So Abby moved quickly back, releasing her aunt and stepping toward the opposite side of Aunty Lili's body.

She'd only been back in Malino for two days. While she hoped to have a boyfriend someday, she didn't need the complication of a man now, and there seemed to be some potent chemistry between herself and Kevin. She hoped it was just the nostalgia she felt for that old crush. Didn't they say your first love always held a special place in your heart? That had to be it.

Abby determined to keep her distance, but be friendly. Kevin was obviously a nice person, willing to help out. He would make a good friend. Especially if he really would help her refurbish the salon for free. She had big plans and she wouldn't be able to handle them on her own.

"So, what do you need done?" Kevin looked around the room. "Painting?"

Ah, he's smart too, Abby thought. He knew just the

right moment to change the subject. Things had been getting way too sentimental.

"Definitely painting." Abby scrunched her nose at the walls. "And not pink, either," she added.

Kevin glanced again at the faded walls. "Isn't pink a good color for a beauty parlor?"

"'Beauty parlor?' What are you, stuck in the fifties?" Abby's eyebrows reached up almost to her hairline. "It's a hair salon. For men and women both."

Kevin seemed taken aback at her vehemence. He raised his hands as though to ward her off. "Sorry. No offense meant."

He looked again at the small room. "So . . . what color works for hair salons?"

Abby had to grin. He was taking her criticism without offense, which boded well for their working relationship.

"I like bright colors . . ."

"Obviously."

The comment was made quietly, but she heard him. She cocked her head to one side and eyed him speculatively. His gaze had been on her hair, but he quickly moved it back to the faded walls. Smart man.

"I thought maybe a happy gold," Abby said. "Or red." She glanced around with a slight frown. "Or fuchsia. That's more purple than pink," she added, thinking he might call her on this after her earlier-stated view about the color.

If he thought her choices too bright, he refrained from saying so. "In other words, you haven't quite decided, huh?"

She had to laugh. "Not quite."

"It's all she's talked about ever since she arrived," Aunty Lili said. "She's changed her mind a dozen times."

"You know what they say." Kevin paused, amusement twitching his lips. "It's a woman's prerogative to change her mind."

Abby watched his eyes, which shone with what she assumed was delight at his own wit. At least he didn't think her indecision was a problem, thank goodness.

When she didn't comment, he walked up and down the room, his eyes skimming over surfaces as he checked the premises.

"So what else needs doing?"

Abby knew what he was seeing. The salon area was obviously located in the covered-over front porch of the old house, with a row of windows across the front so that the hair-cutting activity could be viewed by passersby. He peeked into a door at the end of the long room right near the cutting chair. That led into a small, dark room that housed the shampoo sink, hairdryers, and the patrons' bathroom.

"Kevin does everything," Aunty Lili said. "Painting, carpentry, electric. You just tell him what you want done. He'll take good care of you."

Abby saw the jovial light in Kevin's eyes. Aunty Lili didn't catch the double entendre she'd just provided, but Abby had to hide a smile, and she liked Kevin even more for doing the same.

"So you're an all-around handyman, huh?" Abby made sure to hide her humor over Aunty Lili's phrasing.

"I aim to please." His mischievous grin put a slant on the words that brought color into her cheeks.

Quickly, Abby moved on, anxious to steer the conversation away from the unintended double meanings.

"I know what I'd like to do, but I'll need you to tell me whether or not it's possible. I don't understand enough about construction to know if what I want can be done."

She walked forward, opening the door leading beyond the salon and into the main part of the house, where Patty and her husband had lived. Abby had done a lot of thinking about the house since Aunty Lili first mentioned it to her. She'd only seen it for the first time yesterday, but she'd had drawings of the layout and long letters from Aunty Lili about it. She was ready to discuss her plans.

She was stepping into the dimness of the inside room, waving Kevin forward, when Aunty Lili's voice stopped her.

"I have to get some shopping done, Abby. I'll go, and come pick you up in an hour, okay? You go ahead and show Kevin what you want done."

Without even giving them good-bye hugs, she departed. Kevin and Abby watched her go, Kevin turning a wary eye toward Abby. He didn't look pleased.

"She's setting us up, you realize."

"What?" Abby, distracted by her thoughts on refurbishing the old house, didn't know what he meant. She'd been debating the merits of gold accented with purple versus gold and a deep, bright pink.

"She's matchmaking. It's a favorite pastime for the *makuahines* of Malino. No bachelor is safe."

Abby frowned, and Kevin seemed to think she didn't understand his Hawaiian after her time away.

"You know, the more mature ladies," he elaborated.

"I know." Abby nodded, but the frown remained. Spending two days with Aunty Lili had been a quick refresher course in local language. Although she could speak proper English, Aunty Lili often fell into the local patois, the island pidgin. Especially when she was with other locals.

A steady stream of Aunty Lili's friends had stopped by her house to meet Abby in the past two days, and Abby had seen no indication that her aunt wanted to pair her off with anyone. Most of the visitors were older, of course, being friends of Aunty Lili. But there had been no mention of grandsons or nephews, no hints of setting up meetings, no plans to join someone for dinner.

"Aunty Lili wouldn't try to set me up. I told her I'm not interested in dating."

"And you think that will be enough to discourage her?" Kevin laughed. It was a deep bass sound, and Abby would have joined in if his premise about the matchmaking hadn't bothered her so much.

"Sure. Why not? I'm starting a business. I have a lot on my mind. I don't need complications. And she knows I've had enough of men."

Aunty Lili knew one of the reasons she'd decided to return to Malino was a painful breakup with her longtime boyfriend. Surely she knew that relationships weren't like falling off a horse. In this case, getting right back on––or right into another relationship—was not the wisest choice.

Anyway, why would Aunty Lili try to pair Abby with someone who was so completely different from her? Kevin looked every inch the local beach bum, from his heavily tanned skin to his sun-bleached hair. All-around handyman was just the kind of job a beach bum would have, too, as it would allow him to arrange his schedule around his surfing, diving, and fishing. But Abby was a worker, and she couldn't see herself with a partner who wasn't as goal-oriented as she was. Even if she was ready to date again. Which she wasn't.

Dismissing the subject, Abby gestured toward the wall that led into the main part of the house.

"I guess this was the front of the house when this was a private home." Abby directed him back to the door she'd entered just as Aunty Lili announced her intention to leave. "You'll see when I take you inside, it was one of those old-style houses with two bed-rooms, one on either side of the bathroom."

Kevin nodded. Abby had seen a lot of houses like that growing up; surely Kevin had, as well.

"When Patty closed in the porch for her hair salon, she must have used the front bedroom to create her shampoo room." Since Kevin had already peeked into that room, Abby didn't feel the need to show it to him again. "There's a bathroom in there too, for customers."

"It's a good use of the space," Kevin said. "Whoever did the original remodeling did a nice job."

Abby nodded absently, but she wasn't interested in his opinion of the original job. "What I'd like to do is make this and the living room of the house into one big room for my clients, and maybe open it up more to the room in front. This must have been the original front door," she said, finally stepping through the previously opened door and leading the way into the next room.

They stepped into a musty smelling living room, filled with stale air and gloomy with dark pink paint—the same as that in the salon. Abby immediately walked over to the window, drew back the rose-colored curtains, and opened it. Fresh air flooded in, bringing the scent of the nearby sea. Kevin did the same to the adjacent window, and Abby sighed with pleasure.

"Ahh, that's so much better."

She moved back into the center of the room, all business now.

"Patty and her husband lived here, so she wanted completely separate spaces for her home life and her business. But I plan to use the kitchen and bedroom as an apartment, and I'd like this to become part of the existing salon. So my question for you is whether or not that's a possibility. Can we get rid of this wall?" She gestured toward the wall that separated the shampoo room from the living room, then toward the door they'd just come through. "And this one? Or at least open it up somehow?"

Kevin looked over the room as a whole, then walked back to the salon and the shampoo room. He examined the door between the salon and the living room, then moved along the wall, tapping and listening. He did the same at the adjacent wall.

Abby was never sure just what it was men heard when they tapped on walls that way. But it did look macho, and she didn't mind watching as Kevin concentrated on his task. There was a smooth grace inherent in his movements, the kind of bearing often seen in athletic men and filled with self-assurance. And while that might make for some fun observation, it could turn into a problem when they began to work together.

"You can remove this one without any trouble," Kevin finally said, rapping his knuckles against the wall of the shampoo room. "But, as you said, this wall"—he repeated the gesture on the other wall— "was originally the front of the house. It's a weight-bearing wall."

Abby knew what that meant. She'd have to abandon her hope to remove it and create one huge room, unless she wanted the roof to fall in. Darn.

Kevin saw the disappointment flood her eyes. It was a shame, because he really liked her. Up to now, she'd been looking at everything with enthusiasm and a bright outlook that he found refreshing.

Except for that small cloud when he'd suggested Aunty Lili was matchmaking. He'd bet his beloved SUV that she'd broken up with a longtime boyfriend just before she moved to Malino. Too bad. It might mean that she wasn't going to stay. In order to last in a small place like Malino, you had to have a commitment to the small-town lifestyle. Already, word around town said she was a big-city California girl. Since she'd only just arrived, he thought that had more to do with her appearance than with her actual personality. Some of the men had even started a pool on how long she would stay. Unfortunately, if she had run to Malino on the rebound, chances were she'd be running back to the city before the end of the year.

But for now, he wanted to see the happiness bubbling out of her again. "What exactly did you have in mind? Maybe there's another way to get the same effect."

Perking up, Abby began to explain her hope of opening up the waiting room.

"I want to make an inviting space where people can watch TV or talk or whatever while they wait here. I'm hoping to appeal to the young people, and I thought maybe I could show DVDs if I have enough room for the TV. I can use any of this furniture that's in here, including that big old television."

Kevin liked the way her whole face became animated when she spoke of her hopes for her business. Appealing to the young people . . . Yeah, that might work, what with her appearance. It was hard to picture the older generation flocking to Abby's "salon"—Abby of the spiky hairdo and purple highlights, and a row of pierced earrings along her right ear that ran from the lobe to the upper curve.

She even smelled modern, he realized as she stepped closer to him. The scent that hovered around her had an underlying floral base, but there was more to it than that, something elusive that he couldn't quite identify. Musk, perhaps.

Like the person she was, her perfume was complicated. Surprisingly, he liked it. It suited her quirky looks. Her style was edgy, like her personality, with layers of color, like her hair.

He remained in the doorway as she stepped toward the old television. It was a big console model that must have dated back many years.

"Can you believe this thing?" she asked. "It looks

like it should be on an old sitcom. But it works, and I'm pretty sure I can connect VCR and DVD players to it. It's way too big to put out in the other room, though."

"So you're renting the place furnished?" he asked.

She nodded. "With an option to buy. They said I could dispose of any furniture I thought was too old to salvage. I haven't had much chance to check things out yet, but I thought I'd wait until I have everything set up to decide what I want."

He was happy to see that her eyes were sparkling once more. He took another look around, contemplating the space and what she wanted to accomplish.

"What I could do is make another door for you. Maybe two," he said, using gestures to outline the places he could put them. "That way you don't endanger the roof, but you have easy access back here." He walked around the room quickly, looking at the lower walls.

"You realize that the hairdryers will have to be moved when we take out that wall. There aren't a lot of outlets in there—or in this room, either."

Abby sighed. "I noticed that. It's because the house is so old."

"I can add more for you. And enlarging the room and opening it up to the outer room will give you a lot more light. A different wall color will help too."

He watched as Abby turned in a wide circle. It wasn't a huge room, maybe eight feet by ten, but with the one wall down, new doors and a unified paint scheme it would become a little larger—and appear huge. Abby's eyes narrowed, as though she were envisioning his suggestions. Then she nodded.

"I like it. I think we'll go with the gold back here too, make the whole place seem connected."

He grinned. "So, it's definitely gold?"

She returned the grin. "Maybe."

"Are you going to keep this furniture in here?"

"Like I said, I'll have to wait until all the work is done and see how I want to arrange things."

Together they examined an old sofa, a matching chair, and a wooden rocking chair. Besides those, there were numerous tables of all heights, sizes, and shapes.

As they bent over the rocking chair, Abby's hair brushed his chin. It surprised him to find the strands were stiff but not inflexible, curving along his jaw. And they smelled very nice. Kevin felt a catch in his breath as Abby moved again and her arm rubbed across his bicep. She had wonderful smooth skin, soft and warm against his hard muscle. He was tempted to reach out and put his arm around her, running his hand up and down her silky arm as he held her close.

Luckily, he was distracted by her voice before he could act on his impulse, and it brought him back to the situation at hand. *Lucky* because while it might have felt nice, it would have been highly inappropriate.

"Aunty Lili said Patty liked knickknacks," Abby

was saying, "and that all these tables used to be covered with her collections."

Kevin almost grimaced. "You're lucky she took those."

"Boy, am I," Abby agreed. "Can you imagine dusting all that stuff? Aunty Lili owns a lot of those little porcelain figures and things, and she says Patty had much more. She said it like she envied her some of the pieces."

Kevin watched Abby. She definitely was not a knickknacky type of person. Her look of horror at dusting such a collection was priceless, as was her disbelief that anyone would want more of such things when already possessed of "a lot."

"I guess your clients can use these for watching TV," he said, indicating the sofa and two chairs. "That old rocker is a good one, solid. If you get some older ladies in, they'll like it. But if you don't want it, I know someone who would buy it from you."

Abby bit her lower lip as her mind worked. Kevin enjoyed watching her face as she thought. There were smiles and frowns and rapid eye blinking in addition to the lip biting. Despite the purple hair, she was kind of cute.

"They said I could do what I want with the furniture, but I wouldn't feel right selling something. Not until I buy the place. But you're right about that rocker." She stared toward the front room. "If I could get another one, two of them out on the old porch would look pretty good."

She clapped her hands together with pleasure at the mental picture, drawing Kevin's eyes to them. Her nails gleamed with bright polish the exact shade of her blouse. And there appeared to be little rhinestones glittering on them! It was no wonder the locals thought she was a city girl through and through.

"Can't you just see it?" Abby asked. "The mamas out on the porch rocking and 'talking story' while their daughters sit back here watching a movie?"

She almost jumped up and down as she imagined what might be. Kevin had to grin. She had a great personality, and some good ideas for the place. "Talking story"—just getting together to visit—was an island passion, and the room she envisioned would provide a perfect setting. He hoped she wouldn't get homesick for L.A. and return there. Locals who left to live on the mainland for a long time often felt stifled when they came back to the island. On the other hand, some of them were relieved to return to the simpler lifestyle. Which would Abby prove to be?

"I have a big collection of music videos and movies that I sent over just before I left. They'll be arriving soon. A lot of them are old, but they're classics."

She practically danced around the room. "Maybe I can paint some of these tables and use them. Some batik *pareaus* thrown over the upholstered furniture will brighten the place up and be cheaper than reupholstery." She nodded, apparently satisfied with her decision to use the swimsuit cover-ups as throws. Kevin smiled as he realized she wasn't going to solicit his opinion.

"We can start on the walls first thing," he told her. "Breaking down the one wall and cutting into the other will make quite a mess. Just so you're prepared for that."

"Sure. I'll put all this stuff into the middle of the room and cover it with drop cloths."

Kevin liked her matter-of-fact approach. He'd heard too many women screaming and crying over the mess when he'd helped friends remodel their homes.

"So, what else is back here?" he asked, walking toward the door leading farther into the house. "The kitchen, I assume?"

Abby hurried forward, leading the way to the back. Kevin didn't understand the grimace on her face until he saw the kitchen. Avocado green. Not only the walls, but the stove and refrigerator, the countertops, and all the cabinets. Only the ceiling was a different color—a rather dirty pale pink.

"Yikes."

"Exactly," she said. "Can you believe it? The front is so seventies with the bright pink, and back here it's like we're still in the fifties. The thing is, the appliances are old, but they all work. So I don't want to spend any of my money back here. This is for me, not the public. But it's pretty bad, isn't it? And there's not much I can do without spending a lot of money."

Was there a hopeful quality to that final comment?

Wanting to put the enthusiasm back into her face, Kevin stepped up to the challenge, looking around the room with an eye to what might be changed.

"Of course the walls and cabinets could be painted," he began.

"Of course." She sounded irritated at this statement of the obvious.

"But, you know, retro is in. You ever watch those home improvement shows on cable?" He didn't wait for her to answer him. It was basically a rhetorical question. "You might want to play up the retro feel of this place."

He noticed a spark of interest in her eyes. He should have known someone with her personality would like retro—and something like this kitchen. It was so out, it was in.

"With the avocado appliances and countertops, you could go for white cupboards. Bright, shiny maybe. White walls. Hang some embroidered dish towels out. The place would look like Grandma's."

Abby had started out listening to him with her brows drawn in, her lips in a frown. As he spoke the frown smoothed out, and her gaze began to roam the room, visualizing the possibilities. By the time he finished, she was smiling.

"Sweet," she declared, clasping her hands together

in front of her. She was as excited as a two-year-old with a new tricycle. "I like it. It's so old, it's new. Exciting."

Kevin smiled. He enjoyed making her happy.

"It's a good thing the room is so large, since you'll only have this and the bedroom. And that table is really nice. I'm surprised her kids didn't want it."

Kevin stepped up to an oak table with matching chairs, each of the chairs bearing a stamped design on the back.

"I like that table, so I'm glad they didn't take it. This will be the main room of my new apartment, and I figure I can use the table for doing my books and such. I have a laptop computer I'll be using for the shop," she added.

"Want me to check out the bedroom?" Kevin asked, looking toward the door he knew must lead to that room.

Abby shrugged. "Might as well. I'm going to be moving in eventually, though Aunty Lili wants me to stay with her until all the work is done. It would be much more convenient to live here while I'm doing the renovations, but I don't want to upset her. Still, I don't know what she thinks might happen to me right in the middle of Malino. Has there ever even been an assault here?"

"You'd be surprised." In his line of work, he saw a little too much of what went on behind Malino's closed doors, and not all of it was pretty.

Abby walked around him and opened the door.

"Patty apparently liked pink," Abby said. Needlessly.

The bedroom was—surprise!—pink. The walls in this room were lighter, though, a pale pink often seen in clothing for a baby girl. It wasn't large, and a great deal of furniture crowded the space even more. There was a double bed sporting an old-fashioned, shelf-style headboard. There were two dressers, a shelf unit, a couple of tables, and a mirrored vanity with matching stool that must have been passed on to Patty from her mother or grandmother. It looked like Patty collected furniture too.

"You say Patty lived here with her husband?"

Abby laughed. The sound was musical and made him feel good.

"She lived here as a widow for a number of years. I suspect this room was painted after her husband died."

"How do *you* feel about it?" He had a feeling he already knew.

Abby scrunched her nose. "Pink's never been a favorite of mine, though I like fuchsia and magenta pretty well."

"Hmm. You look like a purple kind of girl."

Abby turned to him, her eyes angry. Uh-oh.

Boy, she was easy to read. He'd made the comment without thinking, because she seemed like a woman who enjoyed wearing purple. After all, she had on a lavender blouse, and nails to match. But he knew she'd taken it all wrong.

"Was that supposed to be a comment about my hair?" Her voice was deceptively sweet.

Chapter Two

"Hey, I have no problem with your hair. It suits you," he said.

She'd been enjoying their time together, and was impressed by his suggestions for the old house. His ideas for updating the kitchen were nothing short of inspired. So she didn't want to believe he was just another chauvinist who would decide what she was like based on her hair style.

Abby examined his face, and her frown slowly disappeared. She nodded.

"Okay." He was suitably sorry for the misunderstanding. She could see it in his eyes. So maybe he really was the nice, helpful guy he appeared to be.

"Kevin Palea, from grade school," she said, her voice soft and dreamy. Too soft for him to hear, she hoped. How often had she recalled the cute little boy he'd been? As teenagers, she and her friends would often reminisce about the boys they'd had crushes on in their elementary years. Three thousand miles away, Abby had never thought she'd see her particular crush again.

"I can't believe we're here together." She shook her head. "In my bedroom, of all places."

"Your future bedroom," he corrected.

"I guess. Still . . ." Abby looked up at him. "I had the most awful crush on you when I was in second grade."

She saw the unfocused expression in his eyes as he tried to look anywhere but at her.

"You don't remember me at all, do you?"

As he seemed to search for a proper reply, she laughed.

"Don't worry, you won't hurt my feelings if you admit it. I doubt too many guys remember little girls from second grade. Especially little boys who were in fourth grade at the time. Boys just don't care about that kind of thing at that age, and they're especially not going to notice girls in another grade. They're into baseball and skateboarding and hanging with their friends."

His apologetic grin made her knees weak. If she wasn't so cynical about men right now, she'd be melting into a puddle at his feet.

"So why'd you move back? Not too many young

people come back to Malino, especially all the way from L.A."

He watched her lips tighten into a line, and her eyes appeared to look inward as she considered his question. He liked that she didn't give him a pert answer and thereby avoid what was really none of his business. She was really thinking it over. He had a feeling her current attitude toward the male gender played into it. But he truly was interested in why she had returned.

As for Kevin, he'd never left because he loved his hometown. He liked the people there and the way they looked after one another—that *'ohana* feeling they'd talked about earlier with Aunty Liliuokalani. He liked that they were not inundated with places like Wal-Mart and McDonald's. Not that he and the other Malino residents didn't enjoy going into Hilo and Kona to shop at those large chain stores. But they liked and supported their small, family-owned stores. The Dairy Queen that had been owned by the same family for the past fifty years. The General Store that was opened by the Youngs when they were newly-weds so many years ago. The tiny branch of Statewide Bank, where the tellers knew your name and didn't mind if you asked stupid questions about how your account worked. The Japanese lunch shop that was on its third generation of Takashimas. The seafood place that had changed owners several times over the years but managed to retain its small-town character and its customer base.

"I guess I became disillusioned with the city," Abby finally said. "Maybe I'm getting older or something," she added with a disparaging grin. "But I remembered how much I liked it when we lived here and I could run around with friends and my mom didn't worry. Where everyone knew everyone."

Kevin recalled those carefree childhood years fondly too. He liked to think that Malino still offered a similar experience to families living there.

"All these years I've lived in Santa Monica," Abby said, "sometimes I did run into people I knew when I went out. But not that often. And the people who came into the salon I worked at in Hollywood . . . they were changing all the time. There wasn't that sense of loyalty that some places get, where the same people come in every month for years on end and you know all about their lives and their families." Abby looked into Kevin's eyes. "I want that, not some woman who looks suspicious because I tried to make conversation while I cut her hair and asked where she lived. Or how she liked her job. Like I was going to go rob her apartment or bother her at work." She rolled her eyes.

"Those are the same reasons I've never considered leaving. There's nothing like going to the school concert and knowing everyone there. Some of the guys I went to high school with are already married and starting families. A couple of the girls from my class"—he saw her raise her eyebrows and corrected himself—"excuse me, a couple of the women who were in my high school class are teaching in the school here. It's nice to have them stay around. One day they'll be teaching my kids."

She knew from their earlier talk that he must be unattached, or he wouldn't have been worrying about Aunty Lili setting him up. But she couldn't resist teasing him a little.

"You have a fiancée and a date set?"

He took her needling well. "No to both. But I'll marry someday, and in due course we'll have kids. It's the way things work. But I'm in no hurry to settle down. I'm only twenty-five."

Abby acknowledged his comment with a slight inclination of her head. "You really do belong in Malino, Kevin. You fit in perfectly with the town. You know everyone, you help out whenever you can. Even strangers down on their luck. Or struggling with finances and setting up a new business."

Her final statement brought a slight smile, but the sides of her mouth quickly turned downward as more serious thoughts intruded.

"I wonder if I'll ever quite fit in. I may have been born in Malino, but I did most of my growing up in Santa Monica. I'm a city girl and I may be fooling myself by thinking that this is what I really want. But

I figure if I don't try it, I'll always regret that I may have missed the thing that would truly make me happy. I don't think I can compromise who I am, though, and force myself to fit the small-town mode."

"You shouldn't have to."

Kevin took in her short hair, standing up in spiky disarray, the tips of some strands colored a deep purple that matched her dark shorts. Once again he noticed the glitter of her nails as the light sparked off the tiny rhinestones embedded in the lavender polish.

He grinned. "You do stand out, though."

Her wry smile told him she knew it. "I figured people would talk about me."

Kevin raised an eyebrow and she sighed.

"Okay. I guess they're already talking." Her smile widened. "But, hey, I am a beauty consultant. I do hair and nails, and I figure I'm a good billboard for my work." She flashed her hands, showing off those bright nails. "And I think Aunty Lili will let her friends know that I can still do the kind of plain stuff they want too. I told her she can have all the haircuts and stylings she wants, for free. I'm just hoping the young people will come in to see if I can help them with the trendier looks."

She eyed him then, concern as well as curiosity in her eyes. The scariest part of starting her own place was the fear that no one would come in for her services. She tried hard to remain optimistic, to plan on adding other stylists some day, maybe even mani-

curists and pedicurists. But in reality, she was terri-
fied that a small place like Malino would not be interested in anything more than basic haircuts—the old
"trim a little off the bottom."

She turned a beseeching look toward Kevin.

"Do you think the teens' parents will let them come
in for trendy haircuts and temporary hair coloring?"

He shrugged. He had no way of knowing. And he
didn't want to lie about it just to make her feel good.
It wouldn't help her if he said what he thought she
wanted to hear. She was starting a business and needed realistic information.

"I really don't know. A lot of the kids color their
hair on their own with stuff they pick up in Hilo or
Kona. You'd probably do a better job. I know Rob
said his sister is green with envy over your hair and
that she can't wait for the shop to open."

At these words, her smile became so brilliant he
felt like he should be donning his sunglasses. He had
to return it, even if his was a poor imitation.

"Really? She can't wait? That's wonderful."

It was obvious that she couldn't kill that proud
grin. Despite the strange hair, she really was quite
pretty. He wondered again what else had driven her to
Malino. He was sure there must be more to it than a
desire to relive her small-town childhood. Probably a
man in there somewhere, but he wouldn't pry into
such a private area. That was none of his business. He

was just helping her out, like the good family friend that he was. In Malino, friends helped friends.

And he could always hear about her personal life later from the local gossip.

"So, what are you going to do in here?" he asked.

"I've been so focused on the business part of the house, I haven't even thought about it. I know I don't want pink walls, though I can live with them for a while." She smiled at him and her eyes sparkled with humor. "I don't think I'd want purple walls, either."

Kevin found that he liked Abby. He would have helped her out even if he didn't, but it would make the experience more pleasant if they could get along. They would probably be working together for a couple of weeks, maybe more, and it was good to discover they could be friends.

"You can check out paint colors when you pick up the paint for the salon. Make a decision then."

"Good idea."

With that, Abby hurried them out of the bedroom. It was close quarters in the room, which was small and held too much furniture. It was warm too, and she could smell Kevin's scent—an attractive mix of citrus and warm male. She should have opened up the windows as soon as they entered the room.

Still thinking of masculine scents and opening windows, she was startled by Kevin's next question.

"So, do you want to start this afternoon, or wait

until tomorrow morning? I can work today, tomorrow, and Thursday."

Abby was glad to return to the business side of their relationship. She wondered briefly what big plans he had for the weekend, but quickly forgot about it as she considered what should be done and when.

"Oh, we should definitely begin right away." She glanced down at her clothes and frowned. "I might need to go change first. When I got dressed this morning, I wasn't thinking I'd be starting immediately. As soon as Aunty Lili gets back, you can go do lunch, and I'll run back to change into work clothes."

The words had barely left her mouth when they heard the front door open. They entered the living room to see Aunty Lili coming in from outside.

"Lunchtime," she called. She lifted three square white boxes she must have picked up at the Japanese lunch shop. "Shall we eat in the kitchen?"

The three of them spent a pleasant hour during the meal, Abby talking a mile a minute the entire time.

She raved about the island food.

"This is so good," she said, her mouth half full of rice from the cone sushi. "You never get this kind of sushi on the mainland. They just don't know what they're missing." She followed up with a stick of teriyaki, licking her fingers with pleasure when she finished. "Teriyaki you can get, but there's still nothing like the real thing."

She also talked about how anxious she was to start on the renovations.

"Kevin says we can start right away," she told Aunty Lili, "but I want to go home and change. These are my good shorts and I need to put on some grungies to knock down that wall. With the new business and all, I won't be spending money on new clothes for a long time."

" 'Grungies?' " Aunty Lili asked. She looked bewildered. "It's so interesting being around young people."

While Kevin tried not to smile, Abby continued her chatter. She told Aunty Lili all about Kevin's idea for the kitchen.

"Retro." Abby finished with satisfaction. "Isn't it a brilliant idea?"

Aunty Lili nodded her head in a dignified manner, signaling her approval. "I can let you have some linens," she said.

Abby gave her an impulsive kiss. "Thank you, Aunty. I was going to ask you if I could borrow a couple of your embroidered dish towels to display. You're so sweet to offer."

Later, in the car driving home, Abby thanked her again for offering her help with the retro kitchen.

Aunty Lili dismissed her thanks. "Ah, if I can't help my niece and godchild, what good am I? Besides," she added, "what am I going to do with all that stuff I have? I'm old, I won't be here forever."

"Aunty Lili," Abby protested. "You're in good health. You do so much, and help so many people. It keeps you young. You'll be around for a long time yet."

"Thank you, Abby, you're a sweet girl. But most young people now don't want that kind of thing. Too old-fashioned. I'm happy that you are interested in having some of my things."

By then they were back at Aunty Lili's house, and Abby sprang out of the car and hugged the older woman.

"Thanks for everything, Aunty. For letting me stay here, for finding the house for me. It's so perfect. I don't know what I'd have done without you."

Aunty Lili brushed off her thanks, but Abby could see that she was pleased.

"You go on and change now," she urged. "Then take the car and go back over. I know how anxious you are to get started."

Abby headed for her room, but Aunty Lili's voice trailed after her. "How did you get on with Kevin?"

"Great." She pulled some old clothes from the suitcase still half packed on the floor, and called out toward the door. "I had good instincts back in second grade. Kevin turned out real well." She quickly changed her shorts. "Too bad those instincts didn't stay with me."

She shed her top and tugged a faded T-shirt over her head. As she headed back through the house, she ran her fingers through her hair, fluffing it out after her fast change. No time to comb it in front of a mirror. But then, that was the advantage of short hair. Finger-combing worked just fine.

Aunty Lili stood in the kitchen, putting away some canned goods she'd picked up during her errands. Abby paused in the doorway.

"So, how come he's just a handyman? He seems so smart, and he looks terrific. You'd think he could find a better job than that. Is he a beach bum?"

To her surprise, Aunty Lili laughed. Not a ladylike laugh, either, but a full belly laugh that had her groping for a chair. She sat down with a thump, still laughing, one arm pressed against her stomach.

Abby began to feel nervous. What was happening? Should she pour her a glass of water? Was she okay?

But Aunty Lili was getting herself back under control. She wiped her eyes with a napkin she pulled from the holder on the table, and hiccupped once.

Abby stood in front of her, an anxious expression on her face, a glass of water in her hand.

"Oh, dear. I don't know when I've had such a laugh." She swiped at her eyes once more. She accepted the glass of water from Abby and took a sip. "A handyman. What makes you think he's a handyman?"

Abby looked confused. "Ah . . . you said he was really handy with everything and would help me out. And I told you I might need to hire someone who could do some things I couldn't handle myself."

"You live on the mainland too long," Lili admonished, her pidgin once again making an appearance. "Here we help each other out. No need to hire someone."

"Okay. So I take it Kevin isn't a handyman." Abby stood with her hands on her hips. "Why is he free to come over to my place on a weekday morning?"

"He's a fireman. They work funny-kine hours. That's why I thought he was perfect."

A firefighter! With an odd work schedule—Aunty Lili's "funny-kine" hours—because of the shifts required to provide coverage twenty-four/seven.

So he *had* done something with his life. Something important too. Admirable even. A wave of guilt swept through her for thinking he'd be satisfied with a care-free, irresponsible lifestyle.

And Abby had to admit the older woman was right about one thing. Kevin was perfect. He'd been able to see her vision. Some men were hopeless at visualizing things like hairdos and room decor. Well, to be fair, some women were too. But many men were unwilling to even try. He'd not only helped her find a way to achieve her vision, he'd said he would be able to implement it.

Abby sighed with pleasure, thinking of her dream coming to fruition.

"I'd better get going. I can't believe I'm actually here, and getting so close to having my own place."

Abby helped Aunty Lili rise and gave her another

hug. "And I can't thank you enough for telling me about the house. And getting them to lease it for so little."

"I told you, we help each other out in Malino," Aunty Lili said. "Patty had a stroke two years ago, and never could get back to work. She lives with her daughter in Kona now. It's a shame to let that place just sit there. We need our own hair stylist in Malino, and Patty wanted to see the house used as a salon again. You did the right thing coming back."

"I hope so. It was a difficult decision."

"Difficult" was putting it mildly.

Abby had had a horrid year. First, she'd lost her job at a trendy salon in Hollywood. Hair by Vi had been *the* place to have your hair done when she started working there. But then Vi lost favor with the in crowd, a newer salon became *the* place, and Vi's was unable to survive the loss of business. It was a story heard often in the world of beauty. Trends were everything, especially in the Los Angeles/Hollywood area. Abby hoped to find something different in Malino. Loyalty, the old-fashioned kind that kept people returning to their hair stylist year after year. That was her wish.

"I'd better get going. I've got to stop at the General Store and get some drop cloths before I head back. I want to cover the furniture in the living room before we start tearing down that wall. It'll be dusty."

"I'm sure I have something in the garage. Let me look."

A few minutes later, Abby was on her way, a dusty plastic drop cloth and a couple of worn sheets on the car seat beside her. As she drove back to the salon, she called her friend Julie Wong.

"Want to go to Home Depot with me tonight?"

"Sure. Time to choose paint?"

"Yep. I'm working on the redo this afternoon. I'll tell you all about it tonight."

Abby couldn't remember when she'd had so much fun. When she arrived back at "Patti's," Kevin had finished his measuring and planning, and was marking out the spots for the new doors. Abby got busy moving furniture, and soon had a huge pile in the center of the room, covered with plastic. She pulled the shampoo and dryer chairs into the front room, and covered them with the old sheets.

Then came the fun part. Kevin asked if she wanted to help with the wall, handing over a sledgehammer at her positive reply. With a thrill of excitement at the anticipated start of her dream, mixed with a dash of trepidation, she slammed the sledgehammer into the wall of the shampoo room. She watched with wonder as that one good whack made a large hole.

"That's some arm you've got there," Kevin commented. "Ever consider pitching?"

Abby grinned. He was joking, but the fact was that she'd done more than consider it.

"Yep." One of Kevin's eyebrows went up. She'd

surprised him. He probably thought she was a real wimp, which just made her grin wider. "I pitched in high school. I ran track in middle school, but the high school softball coach talked me into trying out for the team and I discovered I loved it."

Kevin's eyes showed a new respect. "No kidding? If you'd been in college they would have called you a walk-on—one of those non-scholarship people who amaze everyone when they make the team." He shook his head in wonder.

Abby took another swing at the wall, enlarging the original hole. Why was it men could only respect someone who did physical things? She liked to think she had an artistic side as well, but no man had ever said he admired her for her innovative hairstyles or her creative use of color. Well, no straight guy.

After a third thoroughly satisfying thwack, Abby handed the large, heavy hammer to Kevin. "Your turn."

"Are you sure?"

"It's so much fun, I figure I should share."

"There's nothing like tearing down walls." Kevin winked. "Of course, building something is better spiritually, but this is so much more fun."

He swung back the hammer and let loose. A large chunk of wall went flying. Dust blew and Abby coughed.

"I know just what you mean," Abby said, coughing again.

Kevin frowned. "Maybe we should use surgical masks. We have them at work . . ."

Abby cleared her throat, then sneezed. She took a tissue from her pocket and blew her nose, all the while shaking her head in protest. "Don't be silly, we'll be done in no time."

Which proved true. She took the hammer for a few more hits, and the main part of the wall was down.

She returned the hammer to Kevin. "I'll let you handle the rest of this. I don't want to do any damage to existing areas. I don't want to have to fix things that were okay to begin with."

Kevin took the hammer back with assurances that things were well under control.

"As soon as I get the last of these pieces knocked out, I'll start on the doors. How do you feel about clean-up?"

Abby was surprised that he asked. But thrilled as well. Most men would have just instructed her to start cleaning up the mess, not even thinking to ask how she felt about it. Even though she was the boss at this job.

"I'm fine with it. I'll start right away. Will you be able to dispose of all this junk?"

"Sure. We'll just load it into the truck and I'll cart it over to the dump."

"Let me know if there are any disposal fees."

She saw Kevin nod, but she wondered if she'd ever find out if there were fees involved. Kevin was that rare human being—a nice guy. He might be helping out because of his relationship to and respect for Aunty Lili. But Abby had a feeling he would help out anyone in Malino who needed him. He was that kind of person.

Chapter Three

Throughout her years in California, Abby had remained in touch with Julie Wong, her best friend from grade school. They'd started out writing letters, eventually switching to e-mail. Maybe having Julie, and Aunty Lili of course, living in Malino was what made it continue to seem like home to Abby all through the long years away. Abby had to admit that having Julie nearby had been one of the factors in her decision to move. It had been Julie who met her at the airport in Kona and drove her to Aunty Lili's.

After the excitement of starting work on the salon, Abby couldn't wait to get on with it. She needed a shopping trip to Home Depot, and she knew Aunty Lili's little sedan wouldn't be optimum. Kevin's SUV would have been perfect, but she didn't want to impose. And she *really* didn't want to interfere with his night life. He might have a date lined up, and being the nice guy he was, she had a feeling he would have taken her had she asked. He knew she wanted to move quickly, and that he could only help out for a few days at a time. She didn't want to be responsible for some woman's broken date.

But Julie's family owned a minivan, and Abby knew Julie could borrow it anytime. It was one of the reasons she'd asked Julie to go shopping with her. The other was just that she wanted the company. She'd had a busy social life in California—before Jack had messed that up. So she craved a visit with someone her own age. And she wanted to bounce her ideas for the salon off Julie and get her input.

But as they drove to Kona that evening, Abby moaned over her most pressing need.

"I really, really need a car of my own."

"Want to go car shopping too?" Julie's voice sounded hopeful. Abby didn't know if she just wanted to go look at cars or if she was already tired of driving Abby around. She hoped it was the former.

"Not today. Aunty Lili said she would ask around about a car, so I'm waiting to hear what she comes up with. I'm on a tight budget."

"That's probably a good idea," Julie agreed. "She'll know someone who knows someone, and she'll probably get you a great price. Too bad, though, because looking at cars is a lot more exciting than looking at paint."

"I guess it's only exciting if it's your own place," Abby admitted. She could barely sit still, she was so pumped up by the day's activity. "I walked through the whole house with Kevin Palea this morning. Did I tell you Aunty Lili got him to do the carpentry and stuff?"

"Kevin Palea is helping you? Oh, be still my heart." Julie sighed. "If I come paint with you, will he be there too? In shorts and a sweaty T-shirt?"

Abby laughed. "Hey. Aren't you engaged to be married, Miss Wong?"

"Well, sure. And I love Lenny with all my heart, but that doesn't mean I can't enjoy a fine specimen of a man. Just looking, you understand. And Kevin is well worth looking at."

Abby couldn't argue with that. She shook her head. "I had a crush on him back in second grade, remember?"

"Do I?" Julie rolled her eyes. "And what's this 'second grade' business? You were crazy about him for years."

"Well, maybe."

"No maybe about it," Julie said. "And didn't he turn out to be worthy of that crush?"

Abby couldn't deny it. "He certainly did." She

refrained from saying more, but Julie picked up on it anyway.

"So, how is it going to be? Working with him, I mean? Does he still make your heart go pitty-pat?"

" 'Pitty-pat?' " Abby stared at her friend. "It's going to be fine. Because he doesn't make my heart do that." She refused to say the ridiculous word again.

"Yeah. Right." Apparently Julie could hear the doubt in her voice. "This is going to be fun."

"Now, Julie, you know I told you I'm done with men."

"Yeah, right."

"For the time being."

"Okay. Now that at least sounds realistic. But jerk-bucket back in L.A. isn't Kevin."

"Look, he's twenty-five and he's not married. How great can he be at relationships?"

Julie turned serious. "He's a great guy, Abby. He and Kristy Gonsalves were pretty serious for a while—back in community college. Then she left him to go to college on the mainland and never came back. I think she broke his heart, and he's never been able to find another woman to love."

The melodramatic story was romantic, but Abby told herself she was not interested. Still, it would be good to know if he was seeing anyone. She wouldn't want a girlfriend to be upset at her for taking up his time.

"What about recently? Does he date?"

"Aha." Julie's eyebrows flew upward. "So you *do* care."

Abby, indignant, explained her reasoning about a girlfriend.

"Sure," Julie said, obviously not believing her. "Kevin dates a lot, but he plays the field. According to my brother he's a 'lucky buggah'—always has a pretty girl on his arm. But he doesn't date girls from Malino much."

"Well, good. Then I won't have to worry, will I?"

"Might do you good to get out sometime, though," Julie insisted. "If not with Kevin, I can see if Lenny can get someone for a double date."

"Oh, please, no." Thoughts of a blind date made her cringe. Besides, Julie didn't realize how much damage Jack had done to her self-esteem. How could she date when she no longer had faith in her ability to read a man's character? She'd thought Jack was such a wonderful person. And he'd turned out to be a cad and a loser.

"I wonder if Aunty Lili is setting you up," Julie said.

Abby turned toward her quickly, surprised that Julie and Kevin should arrive at the same conclusion.

"Why would you say that?"

"Oh, no reason. Just the fact that she got the cutest single guy in town to help you out with the house."

"She got Kevin because he's a fireman and they

have those odd work schedules. So he has days at a time off to help out."

"Yeah, sure. She could have asked Lenny. He could have worked over the weekend and taken out a wall."

Abby frowned. "Kevin said she went off to run errands just so we'd be alone. But I don't buy it. She knows I'm not interested in dating."

But Julie barely heard the last two sentences. She'd starting hooting with laughter as soon as she heard that Aunty Lili had left them alone.

"She left you all alone? Just the two of you? For how long?"

Abby's frown remained. She didn't like the direction of this conversation. "I don't know how long we were alone. Aunty Lili had to run some errands. I was showing Kevin through the house, and we talked about the feasibility of my ideas, and all of that."

Julie continued to grin. "Hmm, at least a half-hour, then. Probably more."

Abby knew she'd never change Julie's mind, so she changed the subject of the conversation.

"Let me tell you about the house." Once again excited about her new business and all its possibilities, Abby began to tell Julie about her day. She became even more energized as she elaborated what they'd done and what she still had to accomplish.

Julie liked hearing about knocking out the inside wall. "Darn, that sounds like fun. I wish I could have come over and tried it."

"I'd offer to let you help next time, but we already did all the destroying we're going to do. But you can help me decide on colors," Abby said as they approached the Home Depot parking lot. "Kevin and I measured so I could figure out how much paint I'll need for the various rooms, but I'd really like someone else's input. And you're just the age and gender I want to attract."

Abby practically bounced out of her seat belt, she was so keyed up. "Just think, if I can pick up the paint tonight, I could get started right away. I can hardly wait."

Julie slipped the car into park and reached around for her purse in the back seat. "Man, I wish I had your energy. You've been tearing down walls and I've been sitting behind a desk. Yet you're like a firecracker ready to pop. I feel tired just watching you."

Abby's reply was a chorus of merry laughter.

"So what do you think of this color?" Abby asked Kevin the next morning.

By the time he'd arrived at the house, she'd already been working for over an hour. Tape edged the windows and baseboard, and newspapers covered the floor. A large section of the front wall had already been transformed with gold paint, and a well-speckled roller hung from her equally speckled hand.

The lack of a car was not a problem today, as she planned to spend all day working at the house. Like

Abby, Aunty Lili was an early riser, so Abby got her to drive her over as soon as the breakfast dishes were done. She would have come over before breakfast, she was so anxious to get going, but she knew Aunty Lili would fret if she didn't eat first.

Kevin stood for a moment, contemplating the wall. She liked that he was really *looking,* not just saying it was fine because it was her place and she'd picked it.

"It's good," he finally said. "Makes it brighter in here, but still has a warm feel to it."

Abby stared, concentrating on the sunny color. "Warm as in temperature, or warm as in feel-good?"

"Warm as in feel-good." He frowned. "But don't you dare tell anyone I actually said that."

Abby grinned. "Ah, blackmail material. I'll remember." She offered what she hoped was an evil leer.

It didn't seem to scare him. He merely smiled back and propped the door open. "You're here early."

Abby explained about her lack of transportation and how Aunty Lili had dropped her off after breakfast. She noted an odd expression cross Kevin's face as she spoke, kind of measuring and contemplative, as though he were trying to come to some decision. Abby wondered what that was all about until she heard his next sentence.

"If you don't mind a small truck, a guy at the station is selling his Nissan."

Abby had to laugh. "You think I'd mind a truck?"

Kevin struck his forehead with his open palm. "What was I thinking? A truck would be perfect for you."

She noticed that he took in her hair and earrings as he said it, but somehow she wasn't offended. She knew that Kevin didn't think less of her because of the way she chose to express herself.

"It's a nice truck, one of those small ones, so it wouldn't be much different from driving a car. He took good care of it and it runs well. Just needed something more family-friendly."

"How much does he want for it?"

Abby had carefully budgeted her limited funds, and she didn't have a lot for a car. Her parents had given her some money and countersigned a loan. She was determined not to waste any of it. She wanted her parents to be proud of her, and she planned to put as much as possible into the business in order to do it. A car and her apartment were extras she didn't want to waste money on.

Kevin named a price she was willing to consider. "But he might give you a deal, since we're friends. He's a good guy."

Abby decided she was willing to take advantage of friendship. "Is he another of Aunty Lili's godchildren?"

She asked as a joke, but Kevin replied with a quick grin. "Actually, he is. Gilbert Rezentes."

"I think I know him," Abby said, her voice spiraling upward as she recognized the name. "He's about your age, isn't he? They lived right across the street from us."

"That's him. And he's a bit older, I'll have you know. Lost a lot of his hair already."

Abby laughed. It was fun to banter with Kevin this way. Working with him was going to be enjoyable.

"Gil married Leila Araujo," Kevin continued, "and will be a father any day now. That's why he needs a bigger car. Replaced the Nissan with an SUV."

Abby's eyebrows flew up. "Leila? Really? I knew her. She's a year younger than me. And expecting a baby. Wow."

She and Kevin were silent for a moment, both contemplating their lives as compared with those of friends their age and even younger.

Then Abby put the paint roller into the tray and straightened up.

"So, when can I talk to Gil about his truck?"

"I'll give him a call. But first," he gestured through the still-open door, toward the Durango parked outside. SUVs were apparently popular with firefighters. "I brought the supplies over—for finishing the doors."

"Great. Need help unloading?"

"I can handle it. But you might want to wait on the painting until the rest of the carpentry work is done. Might be some dust, though I can do the sawing out in the parking lot to help control it."

"I know. I did think about the construction dust, but I was so anxious to get started. I thought I'd just do this wall. It's only the first coat."

He nodded, and she thought it was nice of him to pretend he understood.

"You probably should have gone with a primer coat, because of that dark pink. I'm sorry I didn't think to mention it before."

Kevin watched Abby's face collapse. Her brows drew together and her lips turned down.

"Oh, dear. I didn't think of that."

Kevin felt bad about being the cause of her mood change. She'd been so upbeat when he walked in, her face shining with joy and reflected sunlight. Still, he was only telling her the truth, and she'd be even more unhappy if her newly painted wall didn't look right.

But her mood shifted quickly.

She stared at the wall a moment, then shrugged. "I think it will be okay. It's not too bad, and I allowed for two coats." Abby picked up the paint tray and roller and carried them off in the direction of the kitchen. "Let me rinse this roller off, and I'll help you unload the truck. I know you're big and strong, but it never hurts to have help."

Before he could assure her that he could manage just fine, she was gone. The woman was loaded with energy, that was certain. He couldn't believe all that she'd done just this morning. It looked like she was a hard worker. She'd be good for Malino. Small towns were losing too many of their young people, but it appeared Malino had gotten lucky this time. Abby, despite her unorthodox appearance, would be a good addition to their population. She was young, ambitious and full of energy. And her plans were workable ones too, not pie-in-the-sky dreams.

Yes, Kevin decided, he liked Abby Andrews. He just hoped she wouldn't decide that small towns were stifling and flee back to the mainland.

Abby didn't have to argue with Kevin about helping unload his supplies. By the time she'd rinsed off the paint roller, his lumber was neatly stacked near the front door and he was just snapping his cell phone closed.

"So, are you ready to go look at Gil's truck?"

Abby grinned. "Right now? Great!"

Then she frowned. "Maybe I should call Aunty Lili first. She's been looking for a car for me, and I should let her know I may have found one."

She reached for her own cell phone. She still had to switch over to a local carrier, but for now the tiny phone was worth its weight in gold. "I'm still on my old plan, but with unlimited long distance and roaming, thank goodness. I really need to switch it over, but meanwhile the phone company said they should be able to get the land line connected by Friday."

"Do you have a phone for the house? Patty left a lot of furniture, but I didn't see a phone."

"Just as well. They were probably pink," Abby said, scrunching up her nose.

They exchanged smiles, certain of the truth of her statement. But Abby's amusement vanished quickly once she got Aunty Lili on the line. While she was glad Abby had a good possibility lined up, Aunty Lili had some qualms about her driving a truck.

"So unladylike," she said.

Abby had to stifle a giggle. She'd never thought of herself as a "lady"—at least not the way Aunty Lili defined the term. She'd been a tomboy as a child, and a teenage athlete who followed the trendy looks that came and went with such regularity.

She explained to Aunty that Kevin thought the truck a worthy piece of equipment, and Aunty Lili seemed reassured.

"Okay then. I've asked around, but no mo' cars for sale right now. Hard times, people making do. Lucky thing he found you dis."

Abby had to smile at Aunty's lapse into pidgin.

"I'll see you tonight. Maybe I'll be driving myself home," she added, with a grin and a wink for Kevin.

She almost bounced down the sidewalk toward his Durango, pulling open the passenger side door long before he could have reached it. Not that she planned to wait and see if he would open the door for her. Theirs was a working relationship, a friendship. She didn't want him waiting on her as if they were on a date or something.

"Let's go," she called out to him, already lowering herself into the seat before he'd even opened his door.

Kevin followed more slowly. The woman had more enthusiasm than any adult he'd ever seen. She reminded him of his nephews, the seven- and eight-year-old terrors. They were never still, either.

On the short drive to the fire station, Abby talked about Aunty Lili's fears for her safety. Gil was working, but he'd been driving the truck to work, a FOR SALE sign in the window, hoping that someone would see it and want to make an offer.

As he drove on the quiet streets, Kevin tried hard not to focus on Abby's squirming. She was such a live wire, and she smelled so nice, too. He still couldn't identify the scent she used, which made it all the more intriguing. Perhaps jasmine, with a hint of musk. And mint?

Abby spotted the truck immediately as they approached the station. Parked at the side of the station's lot, it was a small-sized pickup, clearly once a bright blue, but now somewhat faded.

Kevin knew she'd seen it, because the energy field in the car zoomed up another notch.

"It's about five years old," Kevin told her.

"It looks great." She bounced against the seat belt, anxious to get outside. "I can see myself tooling around the island in that."

Kevin was sure she could. Her eyes took on a dreamy quality as they got out of the car, and he imagined she was seeing herself driving down the Queen Ka'ahumanu Highway in the little blue truck. He could see it too—the wind blowing through her short hair, making her laughter ring out.

Gil came forward, quickly followed by the other two firemen on duty. Kevin made the introductions, noting the contemplative looks that passed from the three men to Abby, then back to him. He also spotted the quick glances at her hair. He wondered if they'd seen her nails. This morning they were blue, to match her shirt, and instead of rhinestones, there were tiny white flowers painted on them.

Once the introductions were over, and the usual questions about relatives were dispensed with, they all trooped over to the truck.

Gil explained its features. "It's been a good car, but now that the wife's expecting, I needed to get something more family friendly."

Unlike Gil, Kevin noticed Abby's eyebrows rise at "the wife," but she remained silent. Kevin was busy wondering how he could deflect the comments he knew he'd be hearing from the guys later about his friendship with Abby. He could see the speculation in the eyes of his colleagues as they observed the interaction between the two of them.

Despite her strange hair, Abby was an attractive woman, with a shape many another woman would envy. And any man could admire. A shape made all too apparent by the old clothes she wore—a faded but clingy knit shirt that fell short of her waistline, and a pair of worn bicycle shorts that hid none of her curves. He wondered if any of the others were aware of the specks of gold paint that decorated her bare belly.

Abby ran her hand over the hood of the truck. "Can I try it out?"

"Sure. Why don't you go with her, Kevin?" Gil held out the keys.

It was the obvious solution, since the others were working. But Kevin wasn't thrilled about the wink and grin he received from Gil behind Abby's back.

They got into the car and Abby started it up without trouble. She drove out onto Malino's main street and headed for her future place of business.

"I like it."

Abby threw her head back, letting the wind blow through her hair.

It was the image Kevin had so recently visualized, and was every bit as charming as his dream. What he hadn't foreseen was the wonderful scent that emanated from her in the close confines of the warm car. It was a musky aroma, all woman, tinted with a clean smell—like jasmine soap, perhaps—overlaying the suggestion of a warm, athletic body.

Perhaps he was closer than he'd thought to discovering the secret of her perfume.

Abby was enthusiastic. "It handles well, and it's not too big for me."

Kevin tried not to stare. The wind blew her hair wildly about, and she didn't seem to mind. In fact, she seemed to be enjoying it. Her eyes sparkled with gaiety. Of course, with her short hair that always looked slightly mussed, the wind wasn't spoiling her hairdo.

As she laughed merrily at the freedom of having a car again, he noticed for the first time that she had just a suggestion of a dimple on her right cheek. He had always been a sucker for dimples.

He cleared his throat, bringing his thoughts under control.

"Maybe you should try parking it," he suggested.

"Good idea."

She turned into the lot beside the bank, and Kevin turned his attention from her dimple to her hands on the steering wheel. They were delicate hands with long, slim fingers; her nails were not too long, rounded, and, as he'd noticed earlier, freshly painted. She must paint them every night to match what she planned to wear in the morning. He was thinking what a waste of time that was when he remembered what she'd said the previous day about being a walking advertisement for her product—women's adornment and beauty. Actually, she was darned smart. If a man could notice that her nails were always different, a woman would surely take heed.

He brought his head up as she turned the wheel again. Her fingers gripped it lightly, almost gently. It looked like she had a sweet touch, and he really didn't want to think about that. Or about feeling those hands touching him.

He cleared his throat again. Abby was going to think he had a cold.

"What did you drive in California?" he asked.

He watched the little dent in her cheek reappear. At least he was no longer thinking about her long fingers brushing against his arm, or through his hair. Now he was imagining placing a kiss on that spot where the dimple emerged.

He forced himself to listen to her voice, to hear what she was saying. He had to get himself back on course. *Remember*, he told himself, *she's a city girl. She might want to return to L.A.* Though he sincerely hoped she would not.

"I had a wonderful little Volkswagen. The new Beetle. Lime green." She sighed. "I hated to leave that car behind. But it was just too impractical to send it over. And another stylist at the salon I'd been working at wanted it really badly. He offered a good price, so I took it."

"A lime green Beetle, huh? Yeah, I could see you driving that," Kevin said.

Meanwhile, Abby steered the truck out of the parking lot and over to Patti's. She pulled into the driveway, stopped for a moment, then backed out.

"I really see myself in a Porsche, with the top down. But this will definitely do."

Kevin had decided that the best solution to his wandering mind was to watch the landscape. And participate in the conversation.

He kept his gaze locked forward. "Drives well, I take it."

"Yep. And the wind blows nicely through the cab, which keeps it cool."

Kevin smiled. "Your next car can be a Porsche."

Abby laughed, the musical sound trailing along behind them. Kevin knew because as they tooled by he could see heads turning, attracted by the happy sound.

"That'll be the day. Unfortunately, I'm a Porsche kind of girl with a previously-owned-truck kind of budget." She sighed.

"Yeah," he said, anxious to hear her laugh once again. "I'm a Lamborghini kind of guy myself. But we civil servants don't make that kind of money."

She responded as he'd meant her to, laughing merrily as she turned back into the station. The firefighters were out on a call, the area usually filled by the big fire truck bare.

"I guess we'll have to wait for them," Abby said, the regret obvious in her voice. "Or should we come back later?"

"Whatever you prefer," Kevin replied. "Want to look under the hood?"

"Good idea."

She'd vote for whatever would prevent her from just sitting in the truck, not doing anything.

He helped her discover how to open the hood, and together they peered into the engine block.

"The engine sounded okay, didn't you think? Smooth," she added.

"Yeah," he replied. "It did."

They looked for a while longer.

"I don't really know much about engines," Abby admitted. "I can see this one is a four-cylinder, though. And the battery looks new." She pointed to that object, which was cleaner than the parts around it. "That's about the extent of my knowledge."

"Hmm." Kevin continued to give his attention to the engine block.

Abby turned quickly, spearing him with a keen look. "You don't know anything about car engines either, do you?" The edges of her lips twitched as she tried to control her expression.

Kevin slowly shifted his gaze from beneath the hood to her face. He shrugged, offering a sheepish grin. " 'Fraid not."

Abby's eyes remained locked on his face. "With everything you know about construction, I'm surprised. How come?"

"I learned everything I know from my Dad. He loved building things, but he didn't much care about how a car worked. I guess I don't, either. I know how to keep my power tools working," he continued. "But cars get more complicated every year. They're all filled with computers now, you know."

"Then why'd you suggest looking under the hood?" she asked. Her eyes sparkled as an idea occurred to her. "Did you think I'd know all about it?"

The sheepish look returned and Abby felt a glow of pride.

"You never know. You're a rather unusual woman. Tearing down walls, pitching softballs."

They grinned at each other, then Abby began to laugh. "When your car breaks down, do you stop and peer under the hood?"

He wondered if he looked as ridiculous as he felt. "Sure."

She continued to laugh. "The macho thing, huh?"

His shoulders pulled sharply back. "Not necessarily. It's what people do."

"Yeah." Her amusement quieted to a wide smile. "I do the same thing."

"You never know," he said. "Something obvious might stick out."

She nodded solemnly. "Like a wire just hanging there, or one of the belts all loose or torn."

He turned to face her. "And is it ever one of those things?"

"Not for me. You?"

He shook his head. "Hope springs eternal, huh?"

She nodded again. "Saying a little prayer, then going back and trying the key again works sometimes."

Kevin studied the woman before him. She was perfectly serious.

A little prayer, huh? He already knew she was a complicated woman, but it seemed there was even more to her than he'd so far gleaned. He never would have guessed she was the type to rely on the power of prayer to start a recalcitrant engine.

Before anything more could be said, the fire truck roared down the street, and Kevin quickly closed the hood of Gil's truck. He could only imagine what Gil would say if he saw him looking under there as if he knew what he was doing.

Chapter Four

By the end of the day, Abby not only had a means of transport sitting outside the salon, but also the carpentry work had been completed, and a good start made on the painting. There were now three wide "doors" on what had been the back wall of the salon. The rooms looked larger and brighter. Abby surveyed the space with pleasure.

"You were right about the extra doors. It's so much brighter in here now."

"The new color helps."

She'd gotten the first coat on the walls, and the coverage wasn't bad. It was a little streaky, but she'd planned on two coats, so she knew she'd be happy with the final result.

"Yeah. But that's not all of it. I love the openness of it, with the three openings into the other room."

"You'll have to do something about the floor, though."

Abby nodded absently, still intent on the better parts of the day. Unfortunately, those did not include the condition of the floor. Tearing out the wall had left them with carpet pulled back from vinyl, and a space in between where the old wall had been. Abby was just grateful for the island's single-wall construction, so that she was only left with centimeters of bare space rather than the inches that would have been involved on the mainland.

A knock on the outside door surprised them both, until Abby heard Julie's voice.

"Abby, are you in here?"

"Julie." Abby hurried toward the main door. "Come in. Come see."

Julie was standing in the salon proper, staring around her in wonder.

"Wow."

Abby grinned. So did Kevin.

"Abby's done a ton of work," he said.

"Wow," Julie repeated. "I can hardly believe it's the same place."

"You like?"

"It's beautiful. It's so bright and warm. Cheerful, you know?"

"Thanks." Abby looked around with pleasure and a deep feeling of satisfaction. "I'm not much of a pink person. And that shade was so dark."

"True," Julie agreed. "But, you know, the pink wasn't that bad when I was young. I thought it was so classy to come here for a haircut. At twelve, the dark pink walls seemed elegant and sophisticated."

"Oh, I understand perfectly," Abby said.

Kevin raised an eyebrow, and Abby realized *he* didn't understand at all. It was probably a woman thing.

"I had my first haircut here," Abby explained to Kevin.

"Yeah, so did I," Julie said.

"I was twelve years old," Abby said. "Can you believe I waited that long to get my hair cut? Before that, my mom used to just even up the ends so it wasn't straggly."

Julie nodded as though this made perfect sense, and Kevin appeared bewildered.

"Did you dance hula?" he finally asked.

"Yeah, I did," Abby said.

"Me too," Julie said. "But I used to cut my hair. I just kept it on the long side."

"Actually, I was a pretty ordinary girl before that haircut," Abby said with a grin.

Julie laughed. "You were never ordinary, Abby."

"Well, I was a bit of a tomboy, but I wasn't a rebel. Getting my hair cut off was my first act of rebellion."

"Your first?" Kevin seemed fascinated by the conversation.

"Yep." Abby flung her head back, as though throwing long hair away from her face. Her hair being short, however, it barely moved, mitigating the effect.

"My parents had just announced that we would be moving to California as soon as school was out. It was terrible, as far as I was concerned."

"Man, do I remember that," Julie said. She turned to Kevin. "She cried for weeks. I thought it sounded exciting, moving to the mainland."

"I told her she could go in my place," Abby stated, her voice solemn.

"She did," Julie confirmed.

"The thing was, I was scared to death. I didn't realize it at the time, of course, but I figured it out years later. Here in Malino, I knew everyone, I had my hula *halau*, I had Julie. I was afraid I'd never fit in there in California. So I got a teen magazine and found what they said was the newest style, and brought it in to Patty. She didn't want to cut my hair that short, but my mother told her it was my decision to make."

"Your mom is the best." Julie sighed, perhaps considering how her own parent compared to Abby's.

Abby nodded. She knew her mother was a good person. She'd always been supportive, even when Abby was at her most obnoxious.

"If she was so great, why'd you cause her so much trouble?" Kevin asked.

"Who says I did?" Abby was a bit defensive. But the truth was that she had caused trouble. She hadn't fit in on the mainland, of course, the strange young girl from a small town in Hawaii. Not until she discovered sports, and a place for herself among the other teen athletes.

"Okay, I guess I was a handful. And I guess I still express myself with my hair." She pushed her fingers through her short locks. "My mom still has my long hair, tied up with a pink ribbon." She had to smile as she recalled the color of the ribbon used. "I wonder if Patty provided the ribbon."

"Probably did, if it was pink," Kevin said. "Man, that woman must love the color pink."

"She does," Julie said. "We had her at the care home for a while after her stroke. I think all her clothes were some shade of pink. Light pink nightgowns, dark pink robe, fuzzy pink slippers." Julie shook her head. "I like pink okay, but not that much of it."

Kevin reached out and ruffled Abby's hair. "So, you still rebel with your hairstyles? Is that what the purple is all about?"

His fingers touched one of the purple strands and Abby felt tingles along her neck, just as if he'd run his fingers lightly over her skin. What was going on with that? Hair didn't have nerve endings. How could she feel him touching her there?

She started to deny his supposition about her hair

being her style of rebellion. But then she stopped. Was it? She claimed she was stylish, and she certainly hadn't been unusual at her last place of employment. But of course, things were different in Malino.

"What?" Kevin challenged her, though his voice remained soft. There was no antagonism there, just an honest desire to know. "No answer?"

Julie looked curiously between the two of them, but didn't say anything.

"I'm thinking," Abby said, her voice betraying the irritability she could feel bubbling through her. She wasn't mad at Kevin, though, just angry that she couldn't decide how to answer his question.

"I've never thought of it that way," she finally said. "But maybe you're right. My dad never liked my hairstyles, and I may have been trying to get back at him for making us move. He always said how pretty my long hair was, and how he missed his little girl."

"Did he get transferred? That's not really his fault, you know," Kevin said.

"He didn't really transfer. He lost his job here. That was the problem," Julie told him.

Kevin looked embarrassed. *As he should be,* Abby thought. Jobs were hard to come by in Malino, and her father had done what he felt was right. Not that she'd thought that way at the age of twelve.

She sighed. "I know it wasn't his fault, but when you're twelve, it's got to be your parents' fault. The thing was, he lost his job and couldn't find another one. And my uncle in California told him to come, there were jobs where he was working. And there were. We had a nice life there. I just kept thinking we should have stayed."

"And she did let her hair grow out for a while," Julie told him. "Didn't you have it long the last couple of years? Shoulder length?"

Yes, she had. Jack liked long hair, and like a fool, she'd tried to make him happy. She'd even kept the highlights limited to red or blonde, because he didn't like "odd" hair colors. She should have realized that a man had to love the person you were, not the person he wanted you to be.

Looking in the mirror, she ran her fingers through her short hair, gazing with satisfaction at the touches of purple as she fluffed it out.

"I did let it grow out some. But I look better with short hair." She attempted a smile, ashamed to admit she'd cut it all off in pique when Jack told her he'd fallen in love with someone else. "It goes better with the shape of my face," she explained, "and the length of my neck. Take my word for it. I'm a professional, so I know about these things."

Kevin and Julie laughed.

"Enough about my hair," Abby declared. She turned to Julie. "Come outside and see my new truck."

"Truck? You got a truck?" Julie rushed after her, questions tumbling forth as she chased her friend.

* * *

Delighted to have her own transportation, Abby drove back to the salon after dinner. Aunty Liliuokalani fussed about her being there alone after dark, but Abby dismissed her fears.

"Honestly, Aunty Lili, it's perfectly safe. All of Malino is. And I'll leave all the lights on. The people at the Dairy Queen will be able to see what's going on. No one would try to rob a place that isn't even open yet."

"Okay." Aunty's expression didn't relax any. Abby hadn't expected it to. She was a worrier, plain and simple.

"You know, once I open, I'll be doing most of my business in the evenings. That's when women can come for hair appointments. After work."

Aunty Lili nodded. "I know you're an adult, but I can't help but worry."

Abby felt guilty at causing Aunty pain, but sitting around watching TV with her would make Abby crazy, especially when she knew she could be accomplishing something at the salon. And if Aunty wasn't worrying about her, she'd find someone else to agonize over. It was her nature.

But Abby did feel better when Aunty Lili sent her off with a hug and a kiss.

A few minutes later, Abby parked beside the house and proudly let herself into her own salon. It might still be a mess, but one day soon it would be a place the women of Malino would want to visit.

Mindful of her promise to Aunty Lili, Abby turned on all the lights. Then she stood still for a moment, looking around her at the golden walls. It wasn't hard to imagine them unstreaked and glowing with reflected sunlight. Or to visualize them decorated with posters, the furniture covered with bright-colored throws and brighter pillows.

Oh, she couldn't wait! But for now, there was work to be done.

Resisting the urge to continue painting, Abby walked purposefully into the living room and pulled the plastic tarp from the pile of furniture. Anxious as she was to complete the walls, she was afraid she wouldn't do a good job working under the artificial light.

So she would get on with another important job. She had to sort through the furniture she'd acquired with the house, and try to determine what might be useful. She'd also have to decide just how she'd arrange everything, then she could think about extras like pictures for the walls and a plant or two.

The furniture was scattered in a rough circle, Abby standing in the center of it all, when she was surprised by the sound of the door opening. Could Julie have driven by and seen the lights?

She'd barely turned when she heard Kevin's voice. "Hey."

He strolled casually into the room, looking good in khaki shorts and a much-washed T-shirt.

"You should have this locked at night."

"Kevin." Abby was delighted to discover the benefits of the new doors he'd cut for her. Besides the advantages of easier access and more light, they gave her a good view into the salon. "What are you doing here?"

"I should say I was just driving by." His sheepish expression led Abby to suspect the truth before his next sentence confirmed it. "But the truth is, Aunty Lili called and asked me to check up on you."

Guilt rushed through her. "She told me she was worried when I said I was coming over here to work. But she has to realize that I'm going to be living here. I would have moved in already, but she would go crazy if I did that before everything is ready."

"She might have driven down herself if I didn't promise to stop by," Kevin offered as a form of apology. "How about I go over to the Dairy Queen and get us some drinks?"

Abby smiled her thanks. "That would be great. Let me give you some money." She turned, looking for her purse. Then she remembered she'd left it at Aunty Lili's, just bringing her driver's license, car keys and cell phone, distributed throughout the various pockets of her calf-length cargo pants.

Luckily, Kevin held up a hand. "My treat, okay? I know you're not thrilled about me being here, so I'm bribing my way into your good graces."

"You don't have to do that. I'm not blaming you."

She grinned. "But thanks. I just realized I didn't bring my purse, only the car keys and phone."

He grinned back, winking at her as he left.

She watched him cross the street toward the Dairy Queen. It was too dark to make out his features, but his profile was well worth watching. Tall and well-proportioned, he walked with a confidence that drew the eye. She noticed a table full of teenage girls observing him too, their giggles carrying well beyond the fingers that covered their mouths as they leaned in, heads close; the cheerful sound traveled across the street and through her open windows.

Once Kevin was out of sight at the order window, she went back to work. Not that it was easy to concentrate on furniture, though, waiting for Kevin to return. She pulled a small table toward the rocking chair, looking it over carefully, but barely registering its size or height.

When she heard the door open again, she tensed slightly, relaxing at the sound of Kevin's voice calling out to her. She hoped she wasn't catching Aunty Lili's anxiousness. But she thought her particular brand of nervousness had more to do with a certain male presence than with any concern for her safety.

"Here you go." He handed her a tall, cold cup of soda, the straw already protruding through the plastic lid.

"So what are you doing here?" He gestured at the

furniture littering the room. "Planning what you're going to use?"

"A gold star for the gentleman." She took a long sip of her soda. "Mmm, that's good. Thanks. And yes, that's exactly what I'm doing. I'm trying to decide what I can use, and how I'll arrange things. I don't think I'll want all of this furniture."

"There are a lot of tables here. But isn't it a little early for that yet?"

"Maybe. But I'm so anxious to get going, and I don't want to paint at night. The light in here isn't that good." She saw him nod his agreement. "So I thought this would be something to keep me busy."

He looked at her curiously. "You didn't consider going to bed early and resting up after all the work you've already done?"

Abby was incredulous. "Go to bed early when there's so much to do here?"

Kevin examined her face for a full minute, then seemed to come to some decision. He shook his head slightly, as though talking to himself, then pointed to the small table she'd so recently set beside the rocker.

"So what are you planning for this table?"

Abby turned her attention back to the table and chair.

"I'm going to put this rocking chair in the outside room." She threw her arm out in the direction of the outer room. "Like you suggested. That was a good idea. I'm looking for a table to go beside the rocker. And if I can turn up another rocker, then it can go between the two of them," she added. "I can put magazines on the table, and have it available for glasses of water, or cups of coffee."

"You're going to serve coffee?"

Abby seemed surprised by the question. "Sure. Salons always offer drinks to the clients. Some of the salons in L.A. serve wine."

Kevin shook his head. "Wow. I have a lot to learn about salons."

Abby laughed. She was glad he'd stopped by. She hadn't realized how little laughter there had been in her life during her two years with Jack. It was only recently that she was rediscovering herself, and realizing how much better off she was without him.

"I'll just have hot and cold water available. Instant coffee and tea bags—that kind of thing. It's nice to have something to offer when a woman is sitting under the hairdryer or waiting for her color to set."

Kevin considered the furniture around them while she talked. As she finished her sentence, he pulled another table forward, placing it on the opposite side of the rocker.

"Look at this one. It might be a better height."

Abby squinted at the three pieces of furniture for a moment, finally deciding that he was correct. The second table *was* a better height for the rocker. It also boasted more surface area, which would be good for the use she had in mind.

"It's much better." She jotted on a sticky note and stuck it to the top of the table. "So I don't forget which is which."

Kevin nodded, an amused smile tilting his lips.

Kevin was still looking at the assortment of tables when she straightened up, so she could examine him for a moment without him noticing. Aunty Lili might have sent him over, but he seemed perfectly comfortable being there. He'd looked at her furniture and chosen the table knowing it would work better for her purposes; yet he'd presented it to her as a mere possibility. She'd already seen some of that in him—his willingness to let her take the lead. It was only proper, of course, since it was her enterprise. Still, she was impressed. Jack had always tried to tell her how to do things, whether or not he had the knowledge to support his decisions. And he hadn't liked it when she didn't follow along. But, even on their short acquaintance, she knew that Kevin would be satisfied with whatever choice she made.

Shaking off her contemplative mood, Abby indicated the larger pieces of furniture she'd pushed together.

"Planning the arrangement in here is easier, because the coffee table and end tables were already paired up with the sofa and chairs."

She eyed the rocking chair and table again. "So, do you think it would be too weird to paint the rocker and table bright colors?"

Kevin thought it over. "Bright colors like what?"

Abby went into the front room and dug into one of the bags with the paint supplies. She returned with a handful of the sample cards available at hardware stores to help people decide on paint colors.

"Have you ever looked at these paint sample cards? There are some of the most wonderful colors." She sorted through the cards, shuffling them in her hands like a child with a new game.

"I was thinking of a deep red or pink. Something like this." She spread the cards out on the top of one of the tables. "And they have the most wonderful names. The wall color is 'mango tango.' I could make the place a fruit bowl. See, here's 'cranberry tempest,' and 'raspberry royale.' And 'plum tart.'" She pointed to still another card. "This one sounds almost sinful—'passion red.' Don't you love it?"

Kevin looked over the cards, agreeing that the colors she'd chosen all seemed to coordinate. "You should go for it," he said. "It'll be uniquely you. And that's probably the best way to go. After all, Patty did it with all her pink."

"I hadn't thought of it that way." Abby mused over her ideas, staring at first one table then another.

"I'll leave the wood finish in here, but I'll paint the

things in the outer room." She turned to Kevin. "What do you think?"

"Sounds good to me."

Kevin watched her smile at his agreement. He liked to make her smile, and he loved hearing her laugh. He found her enchantment over the paint colors delightful. Aunty's call had pulled him away from a playoff game, but he didn't even care. He could catch up on the score later. At present, he couldn't imagine a better way to spend the evening.

And if the guys ever found out about this, he'd never live it down.

Wanting to get his mind off of Abby's pretty lips, which bowed up at the sides, he gestured toward the two large windows on the side wall.

"What are you going to do about the windows?"

Abby frowned. She seemed to do that a lot when she was thinking. *Heaven help me*, he thought, because he found even that gesture cute.

"You shouldn't frown like that, you know. You'll get lines."

Abby's eyebrows flew upward. That was another of her quirky expressions that he found cute.

Then she laughed. "I'm only twenty-three. I won't be worrying about wrinkles—or lines—for awhile yet." Still, she reached up, touching the pads of her fingers to the skin beside her mouth. "But it's sweet of you to worry about me."

"Sweet? Geez, don't let that get around, will you?"

Abby continued to smile as she returned to her concentration on the side wall and the windows. Finally she said, "I haven't thought that far yet. I guess I'll probably make some curtains, because it will be cheap."

"You might want to consider jalousies. With frosted glass you would get a lot of light, and still keep your privacy."

Abby thought it over, staring at the window while her eyes glazed over. Kevin watched, knowing she was imagining the room as it would look eventually.

"It's a good idea." She nodded slowly. "But what would it cost? I have a very strict budget." Her voice was stern at the mention of her money situation.

"I'll work up a proposal for you."

His voice was so serious, Abby looked up. Then he grinned, and she laughed.

"I guess that sounded kind of prim, huh?"

"Hey, it's okay. I know you're operating on a shoe-string here."

"So far all I've bought is the paint, though I did order in my supplies. It's early yet—for ordering supplies, I mean—but I figured it would be better to have things arrive early rather than late. One thing I remember about living here is how unreliable deliveries can be."

"That's true. And it's good planning on your part."

He glanced around the room. "I'll work on the outlets tomorrow, so that you can situate the big hairdryers."

"Great."

"Tell me where you want them."

As Abby led the way to the wall where she wanted to put the hairdryers, she tripped over the carpet edge. They'd had to pull back the carpet in the living room to tear down the wall, and it was still rolled up, away from their earlier work area.

Kevin reached out quickly, supporting her with an arm around her waist. His warm touch made her nerve endings sing. Tingling pulses cascaded down her back, as if she had her cell phone positioned there, set to vibrate and with a call coming in. Her tummy tightened in delicious anticipation, though what it anticipated was not something Abby planned to encourage—or even to think about.

"Thanks," she said, straightening as quickly as possible so that she could move away from Kevin's warm hands. Her voice sounded breathless, and she hoped Kevin wouldn't notice.

"I, uh, hadn't taken into account what removing the wall would do to the floor."

She took another step, finally achieving what she estimated was a safe distance between them, and enabling herself to give her full attention to the floor. She sighed, and creases once again formed across her forehead. Remembering Kevin's earlier warning, she acted quickly to smooth them out, even though she was too young to worry about lines.

"I had hoped to get away with not redoing the floors, but I should have known better." She continued to frown—forgetting about wrinkles—as she looked at the edge of the carpet that had tripped her. The floor on the other side had a vinyl covering like the one in the old salon. It was old and worn, and needed replacing.

"That's what happens when you have such high-falutin' ideas."

Startled, she turned quickly, spearing Kevin with a sharp look. " 'High-falutin'?' "

"Sure. Tearing down walls, opening up rooms. Getting pretty fancy here, seems to me."

The sparkle in his eyes gave her a clue that he was joking with her, especially as he continued his teasing.

"Probably comes from living on the mainland. In LaLa Land, no less."

Abby realized she was having a good time. Getting the place ready was in itself fun, and certainly satisfying. But the easy banter and the laughter she found herself sharing with this man were the kind of playful badinage that made you feel good. The kind that took away worries and left you healthier for it.

She knew that both the wrinkles and their cause were gone. In fact, any lines that remained on her face now were definitely due to laughter.

"Okay, I'm going to have to do something," she

said. "Why don't you help me measure. We'll get figures for the windows and floors, and I'll consider some options for both."

"I might be able to put a piece of wood here to separate the carpet from the vinyl. A kind of threshold, if you will."

They discussed other options while they measured, and Abby decided to spend some time on the Internet when she got home. She loved online shopping—you could check out options, prices, etc., at any hour of the day, and do it all in the comfort of your home.

It was late when Abby got home, even later when she got out of the shower. So she was surprised to find a message on her cell phone from her mother. Surprise turned quickly to panic. It was three hours later in California. Could something be wrong?

Completely forgetting about doing her nails, butterflies fluttering in her stomach, Abby hit the speed dial for her parents.

"Mom," she began as soon as her mother answered. "I just got out of the shower and saw I missed your call. Is everything all right?"

She heard a faint chuckle.

"I was going to ask you the same thing. I called earlier and Aunty Lili said you had gone over to work on the house. She seemed nervous about you being there alone, so when you didn't answer a little while ago, I began to worry. I wondered if you were still at the salon."

Abby expelled her breath in a long sigh of relief. "You know how Aunty Lili is. Nothing's going to happen to me in little Malino. And the Dairy Queen is right across from the house, so it's not like I'm all alone in a deserted area. There's always someone at the Dairy Queen."

"Well, she's never lived in L.A., so her perceptions of things are a little different." Gabrielle was willing to make allowances for her elderly relative. "You are all right, I take it?"

"I'm great." Excitement began to creep into her voice. "The house is coming along. Aunty got someone to help me—for free, can you imagine?"

"Sure I can. Things are different in Malino. And Aunty is the one you want to call if you need something done."

"She got Kevin Palea to help," Abby continued. "He's a fireman, so he has days off when he can help me. I knew him in school, remember?"

"The little boy you had such a crush on in grade school?"

"You knew about that?"

"Parents aren't deaf and blind, Abby." Abby heard the amusement that ran through her mother's words. "So, how'd he turn out?"

"Great. Better than great. You should see him. If I

was interested in dating, I'd think about him, that's for sure."

"Hon." Gabrielle's voice was hesitant. "Maybe you *should* think about dating him. He has a good job."

"He hasn't asked, Mom." Abby sighed. She wondered if her mother, in her quiet way, was reminding her of her parents' main objection to Jack, who had moved through four different sales jobs during their years together. "We're just working together. Friends. Though he thinks Aunty Lili is trying to push us together. Julie thinks so too. Do you think she might do that? After I told her I definitely wasn't interested in dating?"

"You never know with Aunty. She has a mind of her own, and I won't try to predict how it works. She does like to see people settled down and happy, though. She got your father and I together, you know."

"She did? I *didn't* know."

Her mother went on to tell the story of how Aunty had asked her to help cook for a big luau some thirty years ago. "She asked several other young people too, and I kept having to work with your father on things. She'd say, 'Gabrielle and Frank, why don't you cut up that fruit,' and 'Gabrielle and Frank, would you shred the pork?' And pretty soon we found we liked working together."

Abby refused to see a connection between her mother's story and her own situation with Kevin.

"It's so late there." A quick peek at the clock revealed it was past eleven—which meant past two back in California. "Shouldn't you be sleeping?"

"Of course I should. But I'd rather hear all about my daughter's first business venture. Have I told you how proud I am of you?"

Abby could feel the moisture gather in her eyes as the emotion built up inside her. She blinked a few times and swallowed hard. "Yes, you have."

She settled back into the soft pillows and began to tell her mother about her last few days.

By the time she disconnected, she was not only pleasantly tired from the physical exertion of her day, she was filled with contentment from the familial love that she knew flowed around her—wherever she might be.

Still dreaming of her plans for the salon, she drifted into trouble-free slumber.

Chapter Five

Abby awoke at dawn, feeling well-rested and anxious to get back to work. The sun hadn't been up long, but she felt refreshed. And she'd had an inspiration for the windows. While she liked Kevin's suggestion about replacing the old windows with jalousies, she was afraid that would be too much of an expense. But just before awakening, she'd had a vision of the finished salon—with bamboo shades on the windows. It offered a pleasant airy look and would be fairly inexpensive, and certainly easier than sewing curtains. And she thought bamboo shades would look very nice with her color scheme and the tropical theme of her planned throws.

Since she'd called her mother instead of going online the night before, she pulled out her laptop. She could multitask. While she redid her nails, she Googled "floor coverings" and checked the options available, paying particular attention to any prices mentioned.

With almost a quarter-million hits on the topic, Abby was feeling cramped and cross-eyed by the time she heard Aunty Lili moving about in the kitchen. She'd gotten quite a bit of exercise last night, dragging large pieces of furniture around. Unfortunately, she was paying for it with achy muscles this morning. She needed to do some stretching exercises, and maybe some jogging. Just in case, she threw some extra clothes into her tote.

"Good morning, Aunty Lili!" she trilled as she entered the kitchen.

"You sound happy this morning." Aunty gave her a kiss on the cheek as she handed her half a papaya, cleaned of seeds, and a spoon. "From the tree on the side of the house," she said.

"Mmm, looks good." She dipped the spoon right into the soft, sweet flesh of the fruit. With fruity paint colors still fresh in her mind, she found herself examining the salmon-pink, almost red papaya and wondering if "papaya red" was available in paint.

"Don't you think this would be a great paint color?" she asked Aunty Lili, raising her spoon with its oval of fruit until it was even with her nose. "I wouldn't mind it for a chair."

Aunty Lili eyed the spoon and fruit speculatively.

"I like it better for eating." Her voice was decisive. "That red color is the best kind for flavor."

Abby's lips closed over the spoon, and the sweet fruit almost melted on her tongue. "Mmm. Tastes as good as it looks."

She swallowed hastily, wiping her mouth with a napkin. "I hope I didn't disturb you last night. I called Mom kind of late."

"I didn't hear you, so no, you didn't disturb me. And I'm glad you talked to your mother. She's concerned about you being so far from home and alone."

Surprised, Abby stared at her aunt. "I'm not alone. I have you, and Julie." She almost added "and Kevin," but stopped herself just in time.

Aunty hugged her shoulders. "That's sweet of you. But I meant away from your parents. And I know you and Julie are best friends, but I'm sure you had a lot of friends on the mainland." Aunty set down a platter filled with scrambled eggs, toast, and Spam. She gestured for Abby to help herself, then took her seat. "And soon you'll be all on your own. I wish you would stay here with me. There's no reason for you to live at the salon. You could just go there to work, like most people do when they have a job."

"I'm twenty-three, Aunty Lili, and I'm starting my own business. I want to be on my own. Besides, I had an apartment in Santa Monica, so I haven't lived at home for awhile."

"You had a roommate in Santa Monica," Aunty Lili reminded her.

"Rents are so high there, you have to have a roommate. But you got me such a good deal on this house, I'll be able to manage things. That's the advantage of living and working in the same building, you know. Only one rent payment. Very practical." Abby waited for a reaction, a smug expression on her face. Aunty Lili was always practical, so she couldn't argue with that logic.

Aunty Lili had enough of a sense of humor to smile. "So I did it to myself, eh?"

Then she continued, her manner grave. "I got you such a good deal because Patty really wanted to see another salon in that house. Her daughter urged her to sell the house after her stroke, but she wouldn't. She told me she just knew that someone would come along and want it for another salon."

Aunty Lili fixed her eyes on Abby, their brown irises almost black with emotion.

"You were meant to come back to Malino. That house was just waiting for you all this time. Patty said business was good there. And the house holds lots of cheerful memories—for her and for a lot of women in Malino."

Abby chewed slowly, swallowing the last piece of crisp Spam. "I hope so." Her voice was soft, and not overly confident. But she banished any doubt as she finished her coffee. "I'm going to make a success of The Hair Place. So I'm glad to hear it has good vibes."

"So that's what you've decided to call it. Not Abby's?"

"No. Patti's—with an 'i'—was the old style. I'm moving away from that and choosing something more up-to-date. Something unisex. Abby's sounds too girly."

"Up-to-date is good." Aunty Lili watched Abby fondly as she cleared the table. "I'll finish up. You go on and work on your Hair Place. And drive carefully in that truck."

Abby laughed as Aunty gave an exaggerated shudder.

Abby had gotten a good start on the second coat of paint when Kevin arrived.

"Hey, it's looking good."

"It is, isn't it?" Abby stepped back, taking a moment to examine her work. "I love this color. I just hope it doesn't make people look jaundiced."

Kevin gave her a strange look, which she decided to ignore.

"What's that?" She nodded toward a small carton in his arms.

"This . . ." he made a dramatic gesture with the carton, sweeping around the room with it, before realizing he would have to place it on the newspaper-strewn floor. All the furniture was still hidden beneath protective drop cloths.

But he recovered quickly. He put the box down on the floor near Abby and removed a flat square from it.

"This," he repeated, lifting the square and waving it toward her, "is a donation toward the cause. The cause being your new business venture, of course."

Abby, fascinated by his antics, put down the paint roller and moved closer.

"My neighbor redid his family room floor last year. He was going to do the kitchen too, but never did, and now he says he probably won't. So he has several boxes of this, which he says you may have for the miniscule price of a pair of haircuts. For his daughters, not for him."

"Really? What is it? Let me see."

Abby leaned over, reaching for the square in his hand. She examined it with interest. "It's like a parquet floor. And, what? Do you just stick it down?" She flipped it over, running her fingers over the paper backing.

"Yeah. I helped him with his floor. It's easy to do and looks good. Upkeep is easy, too. Would work out nicely if you like it."

"It there enough to do my whole room?"

Abby glanced around the new, large space that would be her salon's waiting area. The flooring was nice, but, given her limited funds, she would have taken it even if she felt indifferent about it. Happily, she found the stick-on squares both attractive and practical. And there was the added advantage that she wouldn't have to make any more decisions regarding floor coverings. She was still dizzy with the numerous possibilities she'd looked at online that morning—carpet, tile, vinyl, laminate. Cork, for goodness sakes, and even bamboo!

"I figure there's enough in the truck to cover the areas where you have the vinyl flooring now. Maybe a bit more than that. But they still make this, so you can get more." He took a slip of paper from his pocket, handing it to her. "I called this morning, to make sure, and got the price for you."

Abby had to smile. "You're learning, Palea. Good job."

Her smile grew wider when she unfolded the small slip of paper and saw the figures on it.

"That's great! Let's go for it. It's a lot less than carpeting would be. And it will be so much easier to keep clean."

"I didn't think you'd want carpeting around where you're cutting hair."

Kevin gave her another of his inquisitive, non-judgmental looks. She did like that about him. Jack would undoubtedly have told her only an idiot would have carpeting in a salon, and not asked her for any elaboration of her concept.

"I wouldn't have carpet under the cutting chair. But I thought I might like it back here, since I'm trying to make this area more comfortable and homey. But this"—she lifted the square still in her hand—"is much better. It looks easy to install, too, so I won't have to pay extra for someone to do it."

"You and I can handle it easily," Kevin assured her. "Shall I go pick it up?"

"Absolutely. And tell your neighbor his girls are welcome to come in anytime. I'll give them the best haircuts they've ever had."

Kevin brought in the rest of the boxes his neighbor had sent, then headed for the store. Abby watched him go, wishing she were riding beside him. She'd enjoyed their short drive in the truck the previous morning. The fresh sea air blowing through her hair. The clean scent of the man beside her . . .

She scolded herself as she picked up the paint roller and dipped it into the tray. She could paint the entire room in the time it would take him to make the trip. She couldn't waste that much time indulging some adolescent need to flirt with a handsome man.

Besides, she was finding way too much pleasure in Kevin's company. She was an independent business-woman. She didn't want to depend on him, yet she was coming very close to doing so.

She reminded herself that she could have done it on her own, just as she was painting the walls on her own. And doing a good job too, thank you very much.

But of course, if she'd done it all on her own, she wouldn't have gotten the free flooring, since that came directly through Kevin.

With her mind going around in circles, she pulled out her MP3 player and fastened the buds into her ears. She needed some good music to sing along with—something mindless and not distracting while she concentrated on her work.

"The walls are looking great," Kevin told her when he returned. "Leave that for now and come on into the kitchen for lunch." He lifted a white cardboard box.

"Kevin, you're an angel. I'm starved."

Kevin ducked quickly into the kitchen, wondering if his embarrassment at being called an angel showed. But having Abby address him as such massaged his ego and gave him a surprising thrill of pleasure. He liked her, and hoped the feeling was mutual. There was always room in his life for another friend. He just had to be sure not to move beyond friendship. He'd decided long ago that he would never give his heart—again—to a woman who could not consider Malino her home. While Abby claimed to love the town and was working hard to establish herself, the jury was still out on whether she would be able to handle it long-term after her years in the big city. He knew there was a pool among the local men—how long would the new girl last? He didn't think she'd heard about it, or he would have gotten an earful about the "girl" bit.

While they ate, Kevin explained how they would go about installing the flooring. "It will take more time than we have left today, though. So I'll get on with the outlets you want, and I'll help you with the flooring on my next day off."

Abby was disappointed, he could tell. But she didn't object, probably realizing that she couldn't do it on her own. At least until he showed her how to go on. He had a feeling that if he started her off today, she would complete it herself the following day. And he didn't doubt she could do it, and do a fine job too.

But he decided to hold off. *It would be easier for two people,* he told himself. Besides, he wanted to work alongside her for a few more days. He enjoyed their friendly repartee, the laughs they shared, and her ability to surprise him again and again. He'd be working for the next few days, and he wanted an excuse to return to The Hair Place. Postponing the installation of the floor tiles would ensure that he'd be back.

Abby arrived at the future salon at her usual early hour on Friday morning. But, even though she told herself repeatedly that she would not think about him, her mind continued to turn to Kevin. After three days of working with Kevin beside her, even Abby's beautiful golden walls couldn't counteract a feeling of loneliness.

There was a lot to do, and she was determined to get most of it done before Kevin returned to help her with the floor on Monday. The walls were finished, so all the tape could be removed. She dragged furniture around, deciding on placement, then lugged it all out to the kitchen so that the floors would be clear. She made long lists of things to be done and things she still needed.

By Friday afternoon, she was ready to drive into Kona for additional supplies. And after dinner with Aunty Lili, she was back at the salon, sanding down tables to be painted.

On Saturday morning, she painted the rocking chair "cranberry tempest" and the table Kevin had helped her select "plum tart." She would have liked another rocking chair, but she didn't have months to check out garage sales, and Aunty Lili didn't know of anyone with a rocking chair they wanted to dispose of. So she decided to substitute a chair from the former living room, a heavy chair with wooden arms and legs she painted "raspberry royale." She would recover the upholstered seat and back later, once she decided on fabrics.

She took a break when Julie stopped by with lunch.

"It's unbelievable what you've done in here," Julie exclaimed on entering.

Abby couldn't hide a smile of pleasure. "Thanks. The more I do, the more I realize that the house was already in pretty good shape. The biggest renovations were the ones Patty had done when she decided to create a salon in her home."

"You mean putting in the shampoo sink and public restroom."

"Yeah." Abby handed out plates and pulled cans of soda from the refrigerator. "And closing in the porch. The things I did were pretty minor. Even taking out that wall wasn't too bad. It was fun banging it down," she added.

"I'm still mad at you for not letting me get in a few whacks," Julie said. Her exaggerated pout had them both laughing.

Abby enjoyed the lunch break. It was great talking to her old friend, and she could finally draw her mind away from Kevin's absence, though Julie teased her about him.

Finally, lunch was over and the trash disposed of. Julie stayed to help with the two-person tasks— removing the old flooring and hanging the shades. Tearing out the flooring was a tough job, but once that was done, the shades went up quickly.

And Julie had more raves once they were finished.

"Wow. The place is looking great. Will you help me decorate my house after Lenny and I get married?"

"Sure. Have you set a date?"

"Not yet."

Abby didn't pursue it. She thought this might be a sore point for Julie. Could Lenny be trying to get out of his commitment to her friend?

She didn't want to think about something that depressing. Instead she looked around her room, its golden walls softened by the light that filtered between the slats of the loosely woven bamboo shades. Fresh air blew in through the open window below, bringing a hint of the ocean.

Abby wrapped her arms around her upper body and squeezed herself. She'd had a birthday just before leaving California. Her family and friends had all come to celebrate—a combination birthday and good-bye party. Just before she blew out the candles on her cake, her mother had said, "Don't forget to make a wish. And don't tell anyone what it is, or it won't come true."

It was such a childish thing, yet so nostalgically delicious. So she'd wished that her new life would be perfect, that her business would be a success. And that she'd find happiness in Malino.

So far, it seemed her birthday wish—that secret wish—was coming true.

On Sunday, Abby attended services with Aunty Lili, then helped with the elaborate Sunday dinner Aunty always served. Aunty liked to invite some of the town's singles to join her, and there were three guests that day. Abby wasn't able to escape to the salon until late afternoon, suitably supplied with leftovers for an evening snack. With the front rooms done except for the floor, she started in on the kitchen. She took all the doors off the cabinets, and began to apply a satiny white gloss.

When she got home that night, she called her mother. She was bursting to update her on the progress at the salon.

"Mom, wait until you hear what I've been doing."

Memories of the birthday cake and her mother's urging to make a wish filled her mind. But the superstitious admonition not to tell anyone or it might not come true was there too. So she didn't tell her mother about the birthday wish, just how well things were moving along.

"I can tell you're happy," her mother said.

Abby heard the contentment in her mother's voice. She knew her mother wanted to move back to Malino once her father retired. She wished they were already back, but for now the telephone would have to do.

As Abby filled her mother in on her recent activity, she couldn't help thinking how nice it would be to tell Kevin all about it. He'd be back the next day to help with the floor. Abby could feel the anticipation build with the thought. Tomorrow . . .

When Kevin arrived at The Hair Place on Monday morning, he was astonished at what Abby had accomplished. Though he didn't know *why* he was surprised. He'd seen for himself all the hard work she was putting into her new business. The walls were finished, a bright, warm gold that should cheer her clients. Light filtered through the bamboo shades in a way that would flatter their looks. She'd dragged all the furniture from the rooms they planned to cover with the new flooring—even the enormous console television.

"You removed the old flooring." He knew his amazement would be apparent, and he hoped Abby wouldn't be offended.

She wasn't. She merely grinned.

"Julie helped me."

"You're an amazing woman, Ms. Andrews." He bowed toward her in acknowledgement of all she'd accomplished. "The walls look terrific. Next time I need to repaint, I'll give you a call."

Abby chuckled. "I'd be glad to repay you by painting your house. Actually, I enjoy painting. As long as it's a color I can get into," she added.

"Don't worry. I won't be doing any rooms over in pink."

They laughed together. He liked the easy camaraderie that had developed between them. He would have helped her whatever her personality, because he'd promised Aunty Lili. But her lively demeanor was a real plus, making him look forward to the time they spent together.

"I see you're ready to get on with the floor," he said, taking in the empty room. "How did you get that heavy television out of here?"

"I'm a strong woman."

He cocked a brow as she raised her arm into the classic flexing position. But sure enough, a small, rounded bulge appeared.

He let out a low whistle. "Whew. I see I'd better watch my step around you."

He enjoyed the sound of her laughter.

"You'd better," she agreed. "But moving large objects takes more ingenuity than muscle. I put it on a piece of that old carpet and just pulled it on out."

Kevin had to smile at her solution. Strong *and* smart. And cute. And she always smelled so darned good. Whenever he caught a whiff of jasmine, thoughts of Abby flooded his mind. And other areas of his body.

"We'd better get to work," he said. He needed the physical activity to take his mind off the woman who was beginning to look more attractive day by day.

The work proceeded well. They established an easy routine for installing the squares, and, once that was set, were able to chat. It was one of the things Abby most enjoyed about their friendship, this ability to never run out of things to say.

The more she worked with him, the more Abby admired Kevin. Not only was he a feast for the eyes, he was also an excellent carpenter, electrician, and general handyman. He was considerate of her feelings, and didn't get bent out of shape when she told him how she wanted things done. Best of all, he asked her opinion.

She was in serious trouble.

Because in addition to everything else, he smelled wonderful. She had always been a real sucker for aftershave or cologne. In Kevin's case, she couldn't be sure he used either; there was a pleasant, manly odor about him that reminded her of the outdoors—of sunny days and the briny ocean, of growing plants and fresh cut grass. It didn't seem possible that so many scent memories could be incorporated into one fragrance, yet all these things alternated in her perception of his presence. She didn't think a cologne could do all that. It was possible that his soap created much of the illusion, and she was seriously thinking of finding out what it was. Would it be better or worse for her to use it herself? To be constantly surrounded by the tantalizing aroma?

Working closely together in the increasingly warm room, Abby decided she had to occupy herself with thoughts other than the contemplation of how great he smelled. She racked her brain for something they had not yet discussed.

"So, what do you like to do when you're not working?"

"I help out friends with projects. I like to work with my hands."

And nice hands they were too. Abby had noticed them many times over their days together. They were strong and competent, yet he was capable of being gentle when he touched her, like the evening he'd saved her from falling face-first onto the floor after she'd tripped over the carpet.

"You must do other things. Swim, surf. Play basketball." She couldn't help but gaze upward at his hair. The proof of his time in the sun lay there for all to see. She refused to believe that he would bleach it artificially; he just wasn't the type.

"Okay. I do play basketball with the guys at the station. We have a basket set up outside. And I also swim, surf, fish. The usual things."

They set several squares in place, their working rhythm becoming smoother and faster as they progressed. *It's going to be wonderful,* Abby thought, surveying the area already covered.

"How about you?" Kevin countered. "How'd you get those muscles you were showing off earlier? You didn't get those cutting hair."

"Hey, cutting hair can be hard work."

"I don't doubt it. But it doesn't create muscles."

She laughed. "No. I belonged to a club on the mainland. I did aerobics and weight training. Kickboxing. The usual things."

"The usual things, huh? Kickboxing?" His voice rose up at his final words as though he couldn't believe anyone actually studied such a sport.

"Have you ever tried it?" she asked. "It wasn't like I was training to do it in the ring or anything. Just a trendy aerobics class. It was fun. In fact, I have to start doing something here, or I'll get fat and flabby."

Kevin couldn't imagine the vivacious Abby getting fat, but this pointed out one of the problems of adapting to a small town after living in a city like Los Angeles. Would she last here in Malino, with its lack of amenities of any kind, much less trendy things like kickboxing classes? The appeal of the mainland and all it had to offer won over way too many of the island youth.

"You won't find anything like that here in Malino."

"Don't I know it." Abby removed the backing from another of the squares. She didn't seem overly concerned. "Hey, do you think anyone would come if I had an aerobics class here?"

"Here? Can you teach a class?"

Every time she did something that seemed to prove she wouldn't last in a small town, she turned around and did something else that was perfectly suited to Malino. A local exercise class sounded like a real possibility to attract interest.

"I don't know. But I have a couple of exercise tapes we could follow. I hate to exercise alone, and not all women like to jog."

"Well, invite a friend to join you then. Whether you decide to jog or use your tape, once you get some customers in here, you can spread the word and see what happens. You should ask Julie what she thinks."

"Good idea. I will." She sat back on her heels, rubbing the small of her back. "I think it's time for a break. My back is killing me."

His back was hurting too, but he was happy that he wasn't the one to call a stop. That was the macho side of him, glad to give her a rest—and take advantage of it himself, as well.

"Ahhh, it feels good to stretch."

He watched, fascinated, as she reached for the ceiling, then bent forward until her palms lay flat on the floor in front of her toes. He decided not to try that, and instead settled for stretching his arms over his head.

"Want to go over to Dairy Queen and have a soda?"

Abby agreed with alacrity. Once there, they decided to have an early lunch.

"We'll finish up in another hour or so, so we might as well," Kevin said.

Besides, he liked sitting across from her, watching the excitement in her eyes as she talked about her plans. She found such delight in getting even the little things done. He'd lost that ability to find joy in the small pleasures of life. Being with Abby showed him that he could rediscover it, if he just took the time to pay attention to the things around him. It was a lesson he hadn't even known he needed to learn.

"Hey, Kevin."

They both turned at the male voice calling out to Kevin. Gil and Leila were coming toward their table, Leila waddling more than walking. Kevin quickly stood, pushing his food to the other side of the table. If he was losing his private time with Abby, he'd at least gain the pleasure of sitting beside her.

"So how's the truck, Abby?" Gil asked, once introductions were made.

"It's great. I love it. And it's very useful while I'm hauling around stuff for redoing the salon."

They talked about Abby's business then, and Leila promised to come in for a new hairstyle after the baby was born.

"Any day now," she said, her longing for the pregnancy to be over apparent in her voice.

Gil appeared ready to agree. "We had to come over here because she had a sudden craving for soft ice cream."

"What, no pickles?" Kevin asked.

Leila and Abby offered the obligatory grins, but Gil groaned at the old joke.

"Will you be taking time off once the baby's born?" Abby asked Gil.

Leila jumped on the innocent remark. "See! I told you men take paternity leave too. Abby knows."

"It's supposed to be really common now," Abby told them. But she could see it was still a tender subject for Gil. She wondered if he was afraid of tending a baby, or if he just didn't want to be stuck at home with a newborn for weeks. Whatever the reason, there was a palpable tension in the air that Abby knew couldn't be optimum for the very pregnant Leila.

"Want to come across the street and see my place?" she asked.

The tour went well. Abby was so proud of what she'd accomplished, her happiness spread to those around her. Gil and Leila made suitable exclamations over the renovations as Abby explained that the furniture was all piled up in the kitchen so they couldn't go in there.

"I wish you could see it with the furniture. A few more hours and it might have been done."

"That's okay. You can show us another time," Leila said, already sidling toward the bathroom. "If you don't mind, I have to use your restroom."

She hurried toward the small door.

Gil sighed. "She can't go too far from a bathroom these days."

"Hey, how'd you feel if you had a baby sitting on your bladder?" Abby said. She might not have experienced a pregnancy, but she'd worked with women who were pregnant, and had them as clients.

"Geez," Gil complained. "That's exactly what Leila says. It must be a female conspiracy."

A scream from the restroom stopped all conversation and had the three of them rushing across the newly-laid floor.

"What is it?"

"Are you all right?"

"What happened?"

Everyone was yelling something different, and Abby thought that poor Leila would be even more upset.

The door opened a crack and Leila's fingers appeared, gripping the side of the door hard enough to leach all color from the tips. Her wavering voice slipped through the opening.

"Gil. My water broke."

Abby watched in fascinated amazement as the cool, calm firefighter she knew morphed into a crazed father-to-be.

"Oh, boy. Come on, let's go," Gil said, yanking the door open on an embarrassed Leila, who was trying to do something about her wet clothing. "Don't worry about that," he told her. "We have to get to the hospital."

"Calm down, brah," Kevin told him, patting him on the back. "You know all about delivering babies. It's no big deal."

"You tell me that when it's *your* baby," Gil said. He turned back to his wife, and practically pulled her from the little room. "Come along. We'll call the doctor from the car."

"Here." Abby thrust a handful of towels at them. "They're all I have here. They're old, but clean."

Leila sent her a grateful look as she scurried after her husband. Six feet from the door, she stopped cold, put both hands over her stomach and groaned.

"Uh-oh, I think she's having pains." Gil sounded close to panic.

Leila came out of it and grabbed Gil's arm. "You have to keep track, Gil. So pay attention. Check the time. And remember, you'll have to coach my breathing."

The scolding speech seemed to be just what he needed. Gil took a deep breath, then checked his watch. Tucking Leila's arm through his, he guided her carefully outside and into the car.

Abby and Kevin stood on the stoop watching until the car disappeared from view.

"Wow," Abby said. "I haven't even opened yet, and already someone almost gave birth in the salon. What a great story."

She saw Kevin give her a skeptical look.

"I know, I know. She didn't *almost* give birth. But her water broke. It's almost the same thing. Man, this is so exciting."

"You might want to clean up the bathroom."

She pursed her mouth as she looked at him. "You really know how to ruin a moment, don't you?"

Kevin was happy to see her smile as she said it. And she did move into the kitchen to get her cleaning supplies.

He followed her, thinking that a drink of water sounded inviting after all the excitement, but stopped in the doorway, gazing around the room in surprise.

Abby, forgetting that Kevin hadn't seen all she'd done over the weekend, ploughed on ahead to the pantry for her mop, bucket, and disinfectant.

"You started painting the kitchen."

Abby, bent over and reaching for the bucket, paused. She straightened up and looked around the kitchen. The newly painted cupboards gleamed a bright white, making the walls and ceiling look even more dingy. "Yeah. Doesn't it look a lot better? And I haven't even gotten to the walls yet. I really like how the cabinets look. Already, the avocado green isn't as bad."

"You're doing an amazing job."

"It was your idea."

"I meant you're doing a remarkable job in implementing your plans."

"Oh." Abby couldn't help the proud grin before she leaned over to pick up the bucket. "Thanks."

Mid-afternoon, Abby stood in the center of the room, hands on hips, gazing around her. The walls glowed, golden with new paint and reflected sunlight. The faux-parquet floor was in, shining and new.

"Wow, it looks good, huh?"

Everyone would know it wasn't a real parquet floor, that it was just stick-on squares from the hardware store. But she liked it, and it gave her a tremendous feeling of accomplishment to have had a hand in the installation.

"Did you try to call Gil?"

"No. I didn't want to disturb him right now."

"Oh, my gosh, you're right." Abby looked suitably embarrassed at suggesting such a thing. "I guess they'll call when the baby arrives, huh?"

"I'm sure."

Abby took a last survey of the room, then made an announcement that shocked Kevin.

"We did such a terrific job, I think we should break off early today."

"I don't have anything planned," Kevin said, surprised that Abby would propose such a thing. "I can stay and help you with the kitchen." Up until now, she'd been obsessed with getting the house into shape, protesting whenever he suggested it was time to quit for the day. No matter what he might personally think of her mod appearance, he had to admire the way she applied herself to her work.

"Thanks. But I'm afraid I can't stay."

Chapter Six

"**Y**ou're leaving? At three o'clock?"

Kevin knew his voice reflected his surprise. And that he was shouting. But he was taken aback by her action. And he *had* to shout because she'd disappeared into the recently scoured bathroom and closed the door.

He was even more surprised when she came out of the room five minutes later. Gone were the faded shorts and T-shirt that comprised her uniform for working at the house. Now she wore a clingy knit top that showed off her cute figure, with a slim denim skirt that ended a couple of inches above her knee. It also explained why her nails hadn't matched her outfit this morning. They matched this one. Which meant she'd come prepared—she'd planned all along to leave early this afternoon.

Abby stopped in front of the large mirror and fluffed her hair. If he was surprised by her desire to leave early, she seemed equally surprised at his reluctance to accept the shortened workday.

"I have to go," she told him, speaking to his reflection, behind hers in the mirror.

Kevin found her sudden reticence intriguing. She was usually more than talkative. Much more. He was curious about where she was going and why she didn't tell him about it. Up to today, she'd been sharing most of her life with him. He'd heard about people she met on her flight from the mainland, about her shopping trips to Home Depot, about her driving experiences in her new truck, about her endless plans for her new business, and ways to improve it—even though she wasn't even open yet.

He pondered the significance of her sudden silence as they walked toward the door. As he searched for a way to probe without seeming to, he saw Julie Wong pull up out front. Abby increased her pace, grabbing up a large duffel bag he hadn't noticed from its spot beside the door.

"I know you still have some things to gather up," she said, rushing out the front door. "You can lock up. Enjoy your afternoon."

And she was gone.

Kevin stood at the wide windows, shaking his head

in wonder. Women! No man would ever understand them, that was for sure. Just as you thought you were starting to know them, they pulled something completely contrary.

He finally decided they must be off to shop. He was still surprised that Abby would leave with work still to be done, but women did like their shopping. As a man with two sisters, he knew about that.

As Kevin pondered the mysterious ways of women, Julie and Abby were on their way to the Hale Maika'i care center, where Julie worked. Julie often shared news of the care center with Abby. On their shopping trip on Tuesday afternoon, she'd told Abby all about her busy day setting up a party for a resident's ninety-ninth birthday. Abby had promptly offered to do the guest of honor's hair for the party.

"This is so nice of you," Julie said. "Mrs. Akaka is *so* excited."

"I'm happy to do it. Anyone who lives to greet her ninety-ninth birthday deserves to have her hair done for free. It must be boring for them, living in a care center, not being in the best of health." The thought of such an existence scared her to death. Whatever she could do to help them enjoy life seemed little enough to offer.

Julie pulled into the parking lot and eased into an open space. "It's the hard part of working here. I do the best I can, but even the women who have visitors don't have them every day. So anyone who stops by really makes a difference."

"It's not entirely altruistic, you know," Abby said as they lifted her duffel out of the trunk, "although I do think it will be fun. This is great advertising for me. The ladies probably won't be hiring me to do their hair, but they *might* mention me to their kids and grandkids. And those are the ones who might want to check out The Hair Place."

"It was great of you to offer to do everyone's hair. Mrs. Akaka was so excited, and I could see that the other women were trying hard not to be envious."

"When you told me about the buzz, I knew I had to do it."

"Sometimes I feel like I'm working with children instead of adults." Julie sighed. "I didn't mention it before," she continued, "but Mrs. Fujita was trying to get some local publicity for this. She thinks the newspaper will send a photographer. It might be a bit of publicity for you."

Abby nodded absently, not certain how much attention would be good, or whether it might slip into *too* much.

Their pleasant mood continued once they got inside. Abby was surprised, but flattered, to have the director herself waiting to welcome her to the facility. And relieved to see no cameras. Several elderly women peeked out the door of a room straight ahead, talking to those beyond them not able to see into the entry.

Mrs. Fujita introduced her to Mrs. Akaka; the guest of honor then undertook the rest of the introductions. For such an elderly woman, she was remarkably spry, moving along rapidly on her walker.

As soon as she'd met everyone, Abby plunged into her work. She began with the birthday girl, the only one getting the full treatment. Abby gave her a scalp massage along with her shampoo, then trimmed her thinning hair and blew it dry.

As soon as the shampoo was over, they moved from Mrs. Akaka's room to the community room, so that Abby's clients could all be together. It was half the fun of a salon, after all, to gossip with everyone else who was there.

Mrs. Mabel Akaka was a sweet woman with a bawdy sense of humor that surprised Abby. Once her hair was done, she sat in an oversized chair and watched while Abby worked with the other residents. Abby asked for suggestions and individual preferences before she styled their hair, giving each woman a special, personal moment.

"This is more fun than we've had in here since Mabel had her heart attack last year."

Abby couldn't hide her surprise, though she did manage to keep her mouth from falling open. "That was fun?"

"Well, she's still here, isn't she? So it was just a nice switch from the routine."

"And we got those good looking paramedic boys from the fire department to come in," Mrs. Akaka added.

There were approving comments from the other women.

"Fine looking men, those firemen," Mrs. Akaka went on.

"Oh, honestly, Mabel," one of the other women said, "all you think about is men."

"Nothing wrong with that, Helen," Mrs. Akaka answered. She smiled, showing a mass of wrinkles and yellowed teeth; but her eyes twinkled merrily, and Abby could detect the pretty, fun-loving young woman she must have been.

"Marian's grandson is a fireman," Mrs. Milho said. She nodded toward the woman presently sitting in the chair of honor.

Abby smiled at her current subject, a thin woman with lovely skin and a sweet smile. Abby was being as gentle as possible with her, because she'd been told Marian suffered from Alzheimer's. Not being *au courant* on such things, Abby decided it best to treat her with infinite care, explaining what she was going to do before acting so there would be no surprises to upset her.

So far, she hadn't noticed any difference between

Marian and any of her other clients this afternoon. Marian was as excited about her new hairstyle as any of the other women. Just a bit quieter.

So the news that her grandson was a firefighter was a topic Abby thought might enliven their conversation.

"Really? Is he a fireman here in Malino?" she asked, inserting a pin into the chignon she'd fashioned with Marian's long, thick hair. "One of my Aunty Lili's godsons has been helping me out. And he's a fireman."

Julie, who had been in and out all afternoon, was currently in the room. She laughed, which should have clued Abby in. "Tell her who your grandson is, Marian."

Marian looked from one to the other, her smile widening. "My grandson. Such a nice boy."

"What's his name, Marian?" Julie said.

Marian smiled again. "My daughter's son. Kevin."

Abby almost dropped the comb. "Kevin? Kevin Palea?"

"Yes." Marian continued to smile. "Do you know Kevin?"

Now Abby had to laugh. "Yes, I do. He's helping me renovate Patti's Beauty Salon. Did you ever get your hair done there?"

"Oh, yes." Marian's eyes shone as she remembered. "Patty did our hair when my granddaughter got married. Such a pretty pink room, and all the girls so happy and beautiful."

Abby muffled an internal groan at the "pretty pink room." *But that's all right,* she reassured herself. *Her* clients would have lovely golden memories.

Abby was standing in front of Marian, checking her hair from the front, still primping, when Marian's eyes crinkled in delight. Her lips followed, turning upward into a smile as sweet as a chocolate macadamia silk pie.

Curious, Abby turned. Her eyes widened in surprise, a surprise mirrored in the face of the man who had just entered the room.

"Kevin," Abby said, just as Marian greeted him softly. "Charles."

Abby's eyebrows flew up toward her bangs. But she recalled Julie's warning about Marian's health, so she didn't call her on the name.

"There you are, Mrs. Kahio. You look lovely." Abby put a mirror into her hand so that she could see for herself. Marian glanced into the mirror, but quickly brought her gaze back up to Kevin.

"You look beautiful, Tutu Malia."

As Kevin greeted his grandmother, he glanced at Abby, raising one eyebrow in a silent query. Abby didn't need spoken words to tell her what that meant. *What are you doing here?*

"Hi, Kevin. I came over to do Mrs. Akaka's hair for her ninety-ninth birthday celebration. And while I was here, I thought I'd give the other ladies a comb-out too."

"Don't we all look wonderful?" Mrs. Akaka asked. Abby had to stifle a laugh at the flirtatious tone she used.

Kevin examined each of the women. It was a small facility, with only six fully ambulatory residents. All of them were in the community room, all wearing glowing smiles and neatly pretty hairdos.

"You're all beautiful," Kevin said, taking time to rest his eyes briefly on each woman, a subtle flirtation. Then he bowed slightly toward Mrs. Akaka. "And happy birthday to you."

While Mrs. Akaka preened at the additional attention, Abby saw Marian take Kevin's hand. Kevin enveloped her hand in both of his.

"There," Abby said, finding it difficult to pull herself away from the little drama playing out beside her. "Did I do everyone's hair?"

She knew she had, but she also knew the women would enjoy telling her so. Which they did. As she listened, Kevin helped his grandmother out of the chair, tucking her in place beside him, his arm around her shoulders. Abby could see how the old woman relaxed, a pure, sweet happiness suffusing her face.

"Abby, are you done?" Julie stood in the doorway. "I've got to leave. A family emergency . . ."

She seemed flustered, and everyone was instantly sympathetic. The women all clustered around her, asking if everyone was okay.

"No, no, no one is hurt," Julie reassured them all.

"My parents were on their way to Hilo for a dinner party. They had car trouble and are stuck out in Honokaa. I have to go meet them and help out, that's all."

"Uh-oh." Abby looked at her supplies, still scattered over the table and counter. "I have to gather up all my stuff."

"You can't stay for my party?" Mrs. Akaka seemed disappointed. "We have cake."

"We'll sing happy birthday," Mrs. Milho said. "We sing it in Hawaiian too."

Abby saw the anticipation on their faces. She hated to disappoint them.

With a synchronicity of thought that she'd noticed more than once during the past few days, Kevin met her eyes. "If you want to stay, I can give you a ride back."

Abby smiled her thanks. "Well, how can I refuse an offer like that? I'll stay then." She gave Julie a hug. "And you can leave right away."

Abby began to pick up her things. "I'll just get this stuff cleaned up. And thank you for inviting me to your party, Mrs. Akaka."

"You call me Mabel, honey. We'll be friends." Her laugh rang out, more like a cackle, Abby thought, but far too joyous to be witch-like.

With the noisy gaiety of the party, it wasn't possible for Abby and Kevin to speak together until the party was over and they were in the car heading back to The Hair Place.

"That was a nice thing you did," Kevin told her, "giving your services that way. The women all felt like beauty queens."

"I had a wonderful time. Thanks for giving me a ride so I could stay for the party. Poor Julie was upset about having to leave. She's been planning this party for Mabel for weeks." Abby sighed. "I should have driven myself, but at the time we made the arrangements I didn't have a car yet and it seemed like a good idea to carpool. And arriving with a friend seemed so much nicer than turning up alone."

Interesting, he thought. It sounded like his gregarious Abby had her moments of insecurity.

"It's no problem dropping you off."

He drove slowly, keeping exactly to the speed limit. He wanted the time with Abby, to talk, and it wasn't a long trip.

"So, why didn't you tell me where you were going?"

Abby kept her head turned, her eyes focused on the homes sliding by. A light rain fell, and the temperature was dropping. She took a deep breath, loving the unique scent of Malino—a mix of tropical plants, rich damp soil, and the brine of the ocean. It was an aroma quite similar to the one that clung to Kevin, the one she thought might be left by his soap. It wasn't Dove, which she used, and it wasn't Dial, which her father preferred. She'd have to poke around in the bar soap aisle when she went to the grocery store to stock her kitchen.

So why hadn't she told Kevin about the party?

She hadn't wanted to talk about her philanthropic venture. It didn't seem right somehow, as if talking about it beforehand would make the whole thing crass and commercial. She'd done it because she wanted to make Mabel's day happy, not for the publicity. But not everyone would believe that.

Finally she shrugged. She'd shared so much with Kevin over the past week, she owed him an explanation. "I don't know. I guess I was a little embarrassed about telling everyone. Like I was only doing it for the publicity, you know?"

Kevin understood. It would be good publicity; but it would also score points for her with local residents who were still wondering about her mod appearance. They would appreciate her taking the time to help Malino's older citizens. If they knew how reluctant she'd been to spread the word, it would be even better. He'd have to drop a few words here and there, see to it that her attitude became known. She deserved all the goodwill she would get when people heard about this.

"I didn't know your grandmother would be there."

"Yeah." Kevin remained silent for a moment. "It's only been a few months. Mom tried to keep her at home, but it was getting too difficult. Sometimes she's wonderful and knows everyone. But other times she doesn't recognize anyone. She gets agitated when that happens too."

"It must be hard."

"It's very hard. Seeing her like that . . . it's hard for my sisters and me, but it just about kills my mom. Tutu Malia used to be such a busy person, interested in everything happening in the town. She did a lot of sewing, and used to make clothes for a lot of women in Malino."

He paused, remembering how his mother had agonized over what to do.

"The worst part was that her internal clock got confused when she wasn't well. She'd get up in the middle of the night and try to cook a meal. Mom woke up once in a panic because the smoke alarm went off. Tutu had put on some eggs and just left them there. Forgot all about them. They burned, the pan burned. It was a mess."

Abby made sympathetic noises that he barely heard. He rarely mentioned his grandmother, but talking about her with Abby felt right. His mother wasn't the only one who felt frustrated by circumstances; maybe he needed this form of release.

"That was dangerous enough, but then she took to going for walks when she woke up. At midnight, or at two in the morning. She'd just leave the house, even when Mom locked it up tight and hid the keys. She wouldn't put on a coat if it was cold or raining. Then she'd get lost and someone would find her wandering around and call one of us about her. Mom finally decided she had to go somewhere where there was twenty-four-hour supervision available."

"She was very sweet today," Abby said. "I wouldn't have known she had Alzheimer's if Julie hadn't told me so beforehand. I really like her. And she was so happy about getting her hair done."

"She is having one of her better days. My mother visited earlier and called to tell me that Tutu was really agitated. I think she caught the excitement over the party from the others, but she was also afraid of the new activity. No offense to you or your ability. But seeing you do everyone else's hair must have helped settle her down. And your manner with her, which was very good."

"Thank you." Abby seemed pleased with his compliment. "I didn't know how to go on, so I decided I'd just be patient and explain everything so there wouldn't be any surprises."

If Abby wondered why his mother called him because his grandmother was agitated, she didn't ask about it. Kevin liked that about her. She might talk a lot, but she did seem to know when to be silent.

"Tutu sometimes mistakes me for my grandfather—her late husband. So it calms her down if I go for a visit."

"I noticed that she called you Charles. I wondered about that."

"She and mom always said that I look just like my grandfather. He died when I was four, so I don't remember him. But when Grandma started getting ill, she began to call me Charles. Sometimes she thinks I am him, but sometimes I think she knows the truth and just likes to pretend."

If Abby found his thinking foolish, she didn't say so. He liked that too.

"She has the most beautiful skin."

Kevin laughed. It felt good, after the serious topics they'd been discussing. Alzheimer's was such a stressful disease. When someone in the family had it, not only were there the problems faced by the others who had to deal with the patient, there was the constant worry that the same thing might happen to you.

And laughter was an excellent tension reliever.

"I'll take your word on that."

"I guess most guys aren't that interested in the condition of their skin, huh?"

"I'd say not."

Kevin pulled up beside The Hair Place, getting out to help Abby transfer her duffel bag into the truck. Abby protested the whole time that she was perfectly capable of handling her bag herself.

She was still telling him that the bag wasn't at all heavy when the night air was shattered by the tinny electronic sound of the *Star Wars* theme music. Abby realized what it was at the same moment Kevin reached for the cell phone clipped to his belt.

"Is it Gil?" she asked, whispering over his hello.

A curt nod answered her question, followed by a grin. It had to be about the baby!

"Hey, that's great news . . . You take care. . . . Yeah, Abby's right here. . . . I'll tell her. . . . Our best to Leila."

By now Abby was gripping his arm, bouncing up and down as she waited impatiently for the news. He couldn't resist teasing her a bit by holding back the information she so wanted to hear. Only for a second, of course, as he closed and replaced the phone. He wasn't mean.

"What, what?" she asked, as he clipped the phone back to his belt.

"It's a boy. They're naming him David."

"David." Abby breathed out a happy sigh.

Her dimple was back. What would she think if he kissed her right now? A little celebratory kiss. A little good-bye kiss.

The thought no sooner entered his head than he took her into his arms and changed thought to action.

Abby came into his arms willingly. It wasn't until his lips met hers that her body stiffened against him. Briefly, the thought occurred to him that she had expected only an exuberant hug to celebrate the birth of his friend's new son. But he had something else in mind.

As his lips settled over hers, Abby relaxed in his embrace. Her arms, initially thrown around him for a hug, moved up his back and her fingers tangled in his hair. Desire pierced his midsection as he deepened the kiss.

What honeyed lips she had. He could taste the sweetness of birthday cake, and the fruity tang of the punch. But unlike the icy punch, Abby's mouth was hot. So hot, he had to end his kiss and step back before he was singed.

"Ah . . ." Abby stepped back too, bumping into the side of her truck and almost falling across the front seat. "Wow. I guess you're pretty happy for Gil, huh?"

Kevin stared into Abby's eyes. She had to know it was more than that. That kiss was caused by a *whole* lot more than happiness over a friend's baby.

"Yeah. I am. But you looked so pretty with that dimple in your cheek. I just couldn't resist."

Abby looked confused.

"Maybe it was a mistake. But I'm not sorry about it, you understand."

"Uh, no. Of course not." Abby scooted up until she was seated behind the wheel of her truck. She felt around for her keys, unable to tear her eyes away from Kevin.

"Okay," she said. "Thanks for the ride. And the help with the bag."

Now he knew she was confused, thanking him for his help with the duffel after her lecture about being able to handle it herself.

"You're welcome. Drive carefully." He shut her door and leaned over to peer inside. "Tell Aunty Lili I said hello."

"I will," Abby said.

He climbed back into the Durango, but sat there with the engine idling until Abby and her little blue truck were well out of sight.

Chapter Seven

Abby had called to warn Aunty Lili that she might not make their usual dinner time. As they ate a late supper, Abby told her about her afternoon at the care center. She purposely left out any mention of Kevin driving her home, afraid of what her face might reveal if she even uttered his name. That kiss they'd shared had been so special, she wanted to hold it close and savor it. Besides, it had thrown another factor into her new life, one she hadn't thought to consider. She wasn't ready to fall in love.

For the first time in a week, she decided against returning to The Hair Place that evening. She'd stay in, and for once she could call her mother at what was still a decent hour in California.

Sprawling across her bed, she used the speed dial on her cell phone.

"Hi, Mom."

As always, her mother was happy to hear from her, and eager to learn about the progress on the salon. Abby was glad to oblige. She told her about the work she'd accomplished, about the paint colors and their wonderful names, and about the new floor, generously given by someone she didn't even know.

"And today, I had the best time. Not only did we finish the floor, I went over to the care center this afternoon and did the ladies' hair."

"That was nice of you. A good advertisement too."

Abby paused, a frown marring her previously cheerful face. "Oh, dear. I was afraid of that."

Her mother's voice seemed puzzled. "What?"

"That people would think I just did it for the publicity. I didn't, you know. Julie told me about this party she was planning for one of the residents who turned ninety-nine. And I wanted to help make her day special."

"I know, honey."

"But will other people?" Abby sighed. "Whatever, I guess it was worth it. They really appreciated the new styles. I wish I had brought a camera to take everyone's picture."

"You can do that next time."

"Yeah." Abby found herself smiling at the thought.

"I do plan to go again. They insisted I stay for the party, and it was a lot of fun."

"And how is Kevin?"

Abby had known her mother would ask about him. Maybe that was one of the reasons she'd called. Knowing it would come up, she'd be able to talk about her mixed feelings.

"Funny you should ask," she said, settling more comfortably against the pillows heaped at her headboard. "He turned up at the care center just as I was finishing up. His grandmother is there."

She paused, picturing once again the gentle manner Kevin had with his grandmother. There was something special about a guy who could spend quality time with a lonely and frightened old woman.

"Oh, Mom, it's so sad. She calls him Charles. It's his late grandfather's name. Kevin says his family always said he looks just like him."

They talked about the sorrow of Alzheimer's until Gabrielle said, "That shows what a decent man he is, looking out for his grandmother that way."

"Hmm." Abby didn't mention her recent similar thoughts. Her mother would jump on it and pester her forever. Too many of her mother's friends were now grandmothers, and hearing about their beautiful grandchildren had brought on a craving for grandchildren of her own. Which meant she was constantly hinting that Abby should find a husband and start a family.

"You should start dating again, Abby."

Abby almost laughed at the way her mother's conversation followed her own thoughts.

"Mom, I told you last time, Kevin hasn't asked. And I haven't had time to meet anyone else."

"Well, when Kevin does ask, you say yes."

"What makes you so sure he will?"

"A mother knows these things" was Gabrielle's enigmatic reply.

"He kissed me tonight."

"What?"

Gabrielle's voice almost hurt Abby's ear as it moved up in volume, and Abby was sorry she'd confided in her mother.

"You must have left something out," Gabrielle said.

"I went over to the care center with Julie," Abby said. "She picked me up at the salon. But then she had an emergency and had to leave—nothing serious, though, so don't worry. So Kevin drove me back to my car."

"And . . . ?"

"And nothing." Abby sighed, then hoped her mother hadn't heard. "The kiss was great, but that was it. Gil had just called to tell him Leila had the baby. You remember Gil Rezentes. He married Leila Araujo. They had a boy and they're calling him David."

As she imparted this news, she realized she hadn't told her mother about one of the other exciting aspects of her day. Apparently the impact of a kiss from Kevin could push other things right out of her mind.

"Oh, that's right, I forgot to tell you about the excitement! I was showing Gil and Leila around the salon, and she asked to use the restroom, and her water broke."

"Almost had a birth right there already, eh?"

Abby loved that her mother's thought process so closely mirrored her own. "That's what I told Kevin, and he thought it was silly. Because she was a long way from having the baby yet, of course. Men are so literal."

"So," her mother prompted. "Kevin drove you to your car, and you heard about the baby. Then what happened?"

"We were happy about the baby. I thought he was going to give me a big hug, you know, to kind of celebrate the good news. And he kissed me." Her voice saddened. "He said he couldn't resist, but then he practically apologized. He said it was a mistake, but he wasn't sorry he'd done it."

Surprisingly, Gabrielle didn't comment. Abby wondered what she was thinking. And what she might be planning. Would she call Aunty Liliuokalani in the morning to discuss the whole thing?

"I don't know what to think, Mom. I'm afraid I might be falling for him all over again, and I don't want to. I'm not in second grade any more. I'm too old for a kid's crush. I have too much to do, and I don't want to mess things up." *And I'm afraid he doesn't feel the same way I do*, she added to herself.

"You just go on with things the way they are, hon." Her mother's voice was softly encouraging. "Keep him as a friend, and work together like you have been. And things will work out just as they should."

"You sound so wise."

"It's just age."

Abby heard her mother's heavy sigh and laughed, with Gabrielle joining in.

They talked for a few more minutes, then Abby said good-night and headed for the bath.

By the time she'd showered, done her nails, and changed into her pajamas, she was so tired she fell asleep the moment her cheek rested on the pillow.

She'd made a determined effort not to remember Kevin's surprising kiss before she fell asleep, but her subconscious was not so leery. Her dreams were filled with remembrances of his arms around her, of the kiss itself, and his sincere words of flattery. *You looked so pretty with that dimple in your cheek. I just couldn't resist.* A small smile curved Abby's lips as his words echoed through her dreams.

On awakening the next morning, she realized that she hadn't slept so well in months.

Abby still wasn't sure how their kiss would affect their relationship when Kevin entered The Hair Place later that morning. Things would change between them, wouldn't they?

Well, *she* thought they would. Kevin, however, acted as though things were just as they had been on Monday morning, BK. Before Kiss.

He sauntered into the kitchen with a quick greeting, moving right on to the work for the day.

"So what's on for today? Painting in here?"

Abby, still reeling from the emotional overload of that heady kiss, stared. She'd worked through any number of scenarios for how this morning might go. This wasn't one of them.

Slowly she looked around the room she'd already finished taping, at the windows and cupboards covered over with newspaper, and at the drop cloth she was spreading over the counters. Sarcasm seemed appropriate.

"No, I'm just fooling around in here for fun." She raised her eyebrows at Kevin, waiting for his response.

He chuckled. "Okay, I guess it was a foolish question. It looks like you're about ready to start."

She nodded. "Just as soon as I get the sheet over the refrigerator."

Kevin moved into the room with the brisk confidence he always showed. "This won't take too long, you know."

"Good. Because I have a lot more work to do . . . cleaning, for one thing."

"Sounds exciting," he said, his tone belying his words.

They had gotten so attuned to working together, he opened the paint cans and filled the trays without consulting her.

"It is. I can hardly wait to move in and start doing people's hair. It will be such fun to have people coming in all the time, asking my advice about hair styles and color."

Just thinking about it made her eyes sparkle.

"The salon is almost ready," Abby said, adding an extender to the roller and dipping it into the tray. She lifted it toward the ceiling as she spoke. "But my apartment still needs some work. I want to wash out cupboards and whatever pots and pans and things are in here once the painting is done."

"I'll help you."

"What?" Abby was so surprised, the roller jerked, leaving a ragged streak of white on the pale pink. She ran it back over the area quickly, smoothing the new paint over the old.

"I said I'll help. It'll go quicker with two people."

"I know. I'm just surprised you'd offer to help clean up."

Abby kept her eyes on her work, but in her peripheral vision, she could see that Kevin was rapidly covering his half of the ceiling.

"Come on, get going there, slowpoke," he teased.

"This is going to be done in no time. You'll only need one coat for the ceiling.

"As for cleaning up, why shouldn't I? I like you, Abby. You're a hard worker. So I don't mind helping you out. And I think having a salon in Malino again will be good for the town."

Abby wondered if her cheeks were turning red. His praise certainly had her feeling warm. In fact, when he said that he liked her, she felt a rush of pleasure that shivered its way down her spine.

Up until now, Abby had considered the kitchen a large room. But that was before she was trapped in it with Kevin and two long-handled paint rollers. They were much too close, their shoulders literally rubbing as they moved to cover the ceiling with paint. The day was overcast, with a light rain falling outside, which made it sultry inside. The air felt heavy, and Kevin's tempting scent filled her nostrils. No matter what they were doing, a fresh outdoorsy fragrance seemed to surround him. Abby hated to admit how much she liked it. Once again she was tempted to ask him what kind of soap he used. She wouldn't mind getting a bar, so she could sniff it in the privacy of her room and remember how sweet it had been to kiss Kevin. And to hear him say he liked her.

Abby was relieved when they finished the ceiling and moved on to the walls. It was easier to put some space between them while working on opposite walls.

But the easy banter that had caused their time together to move so quickly seemed elusive. Abby thought it partly due to the gloomy day. The sky was dark with heavy clouds, so that they needed the lights on. And the misty rain had turned into a downpour, saturating the air with moisture.

Kevin glanced her way as they listened to the rain thunder down on the tin roof. "At least this will assure you that the roof is in good shape," he commented.

Abby agreed, then plunged back into her thoughts. The other reason for the tension she felt was, of course, that kiss. It had been a lovely kiss, gentle and sweet. But now she wished it had never happened. She missed the camaraderie of days past. She hated that they were both studiously avoiding the topic of their kiss, treating it as though it had never happened. Because of course, it had, and it had been a momentous event.

A sudden thought had her stopping her roller midway through one of its long sweeps. Surely she wasn't the only one who'd felt that their kiss was a momentous occasion. It didn't seem possible for one party in a kiss to be so thoroughly moved while the other party barely noticed. Was it? It couldn't be that Kevin didn't even remember it, could it?

Still, it came as a relief to Abby when they finished up the walls and began to clean the brushes and rollers. Until they banged shoulders standing together at the big laundry tubs out back and she got a tingly feeling that traveled all the way to her toes. Wouldn't it just be too, too nice if Kevin were to lean over and give her another kiss now?

As she told herself such an action was sure to bring on more grief, she was startled to hear a phone ring. Pachelbel's *Canon in D*. She realized it came from Kevin's belt just as he excused himself, grabbing a towel to dry his hands so he could answer the call.

Abby concentrated on washing up the paint things, but it was obvious to her that Kevin was talking to his mother about his grandmother Marian. Her forehead furrowed in concern.

"Is Mrs. Kahio okay?" she asked as soon as he clicked the phone shut.

"Yeah."

Kevin's lips tightened and thin lines appeared at the sides of his mouth. Abby felt a sudden urge to smooth over them with her fingertips until they became lost in the larger smile lines that bracketed his mouth.

"Tutu's having a bad day, and Ma thought it might help if I went over to see her."

Abby grabbed the towel he'd used earlier and dried her hands. Then she put them on his back and pushed.

"Go on, go on. You're needed there, I'm sure, or she wouldn't have bothered you."

A smile lightened her mood as she remembered the gentle old woman calling her grandson by her late husband's name. "Tell her I said hello, okay?"

"I will." Kevin was already rounding the side of the house, staying under the roof overhang to avoid being drenched. "I'm sorry to leave you like this."

"Hey, the room is done. It's okay. I'll start cleaning the cupboards and washing the dishes. It'll take a little longer without you, but it'll get done. I'd planned on doing it alone anyway."

She stood under the eaves watching as Kevin made a dash through the rain, got into his car and backed out. She waved as he pulled onto the main road, and experienced a surge of pleasure when he waved back.

There was something really special about a man who would rush off to help out with his ill grandmother. Not to mention one who would actually volunteer to help clean cupboards.

As she began filling the sink with dishes—no dishwasher in such an old house—Abby couldn't help but recall her years with Jack. She'd cooked for him sometimes, at his place. He never offered to help with the dishes, usually just disappearing into the living room to watch television while she cleaned up. She actually asked him to dry once, saying how nice it would be to have him there in the kitchen with her while she worked. He'd never answered her, just gone on about his business like he hadn't heard.

Abby sighed. The more she remembered her time with Jack, the more she felt that love truly was blind. With the distance of their months apart, she could see that there was little to like about Jack, much less love. What a waste of two years!

Abby was stocking supplies at her work station the next morning when she heard the roar of a large truck. Looking up, she realized that the town fire engine was pulling into her tiny parking lot, and Kevin, in full gear, climbed out of the back.

What on earth was going on? She sure hoped the place wasn't on fire. She didn't smell any smoke, but she hadn't thought to check the smoke alarm batteries. Another item to add to her neverending list.

As she pushed open the front door, she noticed that Kevin carried something in his arms. Something small, and wrapped in a dirty blanket. Good grief, was he bringing an injured child here?

"Kevin . . ."

"Hi, Abby."

Abby's attention was distracted by Gil, driving the truck and leaning out the open window to wave. He had a smile on his face, so whatever Kevin was carrying, it couldn't be anything tragic.

Abby waved. "How's the baby?"

His smile grew wider. "Great. Most beautiful baby ever born."

Before they could say anything more, Kevin was standing in front of her. Her attention turned to him. "What's happening?"

"Look what we turned up. Stuck in a gully, poor thing."

He proffered his bundle, opening up the blanket so that she could see. A fuzzy little head stuck out, several different shades of brown, with huge dark eyes peering up at her.

"A dog?" She might be saying the obvious, but she was stumped. If they'd found a dog, shouldn't they be taking it to the animal clinic? Why were they here?

"He needs a good home," Kevin said, "and I thought of you right away. Aunty Lili won't be so worried if you have a dog here to protect you."

Abby looked from the muddy bundle in his arms to his eager face, her eyebrows arching almost to her hairline. "That little thing is going to protect me?"

"Sure. As soon as you fatten him up and he grows a bit."

"He could use a haircut, too," Gil called out. "You're perfect for him."

Abby was at a loss. She supposed a dog was a good idea. She'd actually thought about getting a pet once she settled in, but she'd imagined a shop cat. However, as Kevin said, Aunty Lili might like the idea of a watchdog. Abby hated to worry her, but she didn't plan to room with her forever, either.

But a found dog . . .

"What if he's someone's pet that got lost? I don't want to get attached to him and then have the real owner come forward."

But all three of the firefighters were shaking their heads. "We had Greg out to help when we were trying to get to him."

Abby knew that Greg was the town's young vet. She'd heard all about him from Aunty Lili.

"The people who called said they'd been hearing strange noises all week. Couldn't figure out what it was, or where it was coming from. Finally the teenage boy decided he was going to figure it out. Hiked around in back of the house until he realized it was this little guy. He was stuck down in an inaccessible area of a gully that washes out into the ocean. The boy was afraid that if it rained again later today, he might drown or get washed out to sea. Greg said it looked like he'd been stuck in there for days, maybe as much as a week."

"There's no collar, and Greg checked for an ID chip," Gil said. "He doesn't have one."

"See, the thing is, if he belonged to someone, they would have been looking all this time." Jim, the third member of the truck's team, finally weighed in. "But no one around here knows anything about a missing dog. And Greg says he's young, probably only a few months old."

"He seems like a nice dog," Gil said. "Didn't try to bite any of us, even though we had a tough time with getting him up out of there. We tried to clean him off a bit, but he's still dirty. Could use a shampoo and a trim, like I said."

Abby bowed to the inevitable. Besides, the little guy had already touched her heart with his expressive eyes. She put out her arms, and Kevin deposited the dog into them. She was noticing the warmth of Kevin's hands on hers as they accomplished the transfer when the radio in the truck blared out a message.

"Oops. Gotta go." Kevin pulled his arms back and returned quickly to the truck.

Within seconds, Abby stood alone in front of The Hair Place, a dirty towel and even dirtier puppy in her arms, watching the fire truck zoom down the street, its siren shattering the peaceful morning. Her arms tightened protectively around the dog as he whined and struggled against the loud noise.

"You poor thing," Abby crooned, heading back inside. She was relieved to see that he quieted right down at the sound of her voice. He already liked her! "Let's get you out of this dirty thing and see what you look like."

She carried the dog into her personal bathroom, not certain what a public health inspector might think if she were seen shampooing a dog at the salon's sink.

Once she was seated on the floor beside the tub, she unwrapped the little animal. Then she didn't know whether to laugh—hysterically—or cry. The dog was small, perhaps a foot high and eighteen inches long. But he was painfully thin. His ribs showed through his skin, even with his long coat and the mud that remained on it.

"Oh, dear." Abby wasn't sure if she was talking to the dog, or saying a little prayer. This little guy needed help, that was certain. But why did Kevin bring him here? She could believe that he was tenderhearted. Then she realized what should have been obvious. With his odd working schedule, Kevin couldn't keep the dog himself. And perhaps he *was* just trying to help her out by relieving Aunty's worry.

Her heart broke as she washed the little dog, who was the soul of patience. In fact, any time her face got within kissing distance, his tongue shot out to lap at her cheeks, chin, or mouth.

He was painfully thin, and by the time she'd cleaned him, combed out the snarls in his fur, and dried him off—despite Gil's joking, she was *not* going to give him a trim—she was near panic. Because she realized that she had no food to speak of in the house. A few granola bars, some soft drinks. But no real food. She hadn't planned to stock the kitchen until she was ready to move in. But this poor animal needed something to eat.

She was ready to run across the street to the Dairy Queen to get him a hamburger when her cell phone rang. She didn't recognize the number, but it looked familiar. She hadn't been in Malino long enough to construct a long local call list. Could it be Kevin?

She offered a tentative hello.

"Hey."

Abby was so relieved to hear Kevin's voice, she almost laughed.

"I forgot to leave the sack with you. Sorry. It's some stuff Greg sent. We'll drop it off on the way back to the station."

Abby stood with the phone in her hand, staring at it. That was it. He'd ended the call.

Abby sighed. She'd been a pet owner for all of half an hour, and already it was harder than she expected. But darn if the little guy's big eyes hadn't already won her over. She just hoped that sack contained food of some kind.

She looked down to see the pup staring up at her with those big brown eyes just as she heard the fire truck return. Scooping up the now clean puppy, she ran outside. Kevin climbed out of the truck, much as before, except that this time he held a brown grocery bag. And he was not rigged out in full gear. In fact, she noticed that he looked quite fine in a dark blue department T-shirt.

"Here you go," he said, handing over the paper sack. "Some food, a leash and collar, and a brush. Greg said it's a gift, and thanks for taking him." He winked at her. "I knew you would."

Jim stood behind Kevin and reached around him to pet the dog. "He cleaned up pretty good, eh?"

"He did. Should I call Greg to find out about food and stuff?"

"That's probably a good idea. But he did say not to feed him too much all at once. A little at a time until he gets adjusted."

She nodded, and the men said they had to be going. Once again, she watched the truck pull away from the salon with the puppy in her arms. This time they didn't use the siren, but the pup still seemed agitated when the engine revved up and the truck moved forward. She quieted him with a soft voice and a bit of petting.

"Well, pup, it's you and me. But now I have something for you to eat."

Suddenly, the work at the salon didn't seem as urgent.

She spent the next hour feeding the puppy and fussing over him, then taking him outside for a walk. When she was finally ready to get back to work, she fixed a towel for him on the floor, and gathered up supplies to start cleaning in the bedroom. Every now and then, she'd look over at the puppy. He kept his eyes on her and finally fell asleep.

Abby thought of Kevin every time she looked over at the pup. He was a cute little thing now that he was cleaned up. Abby thought he probably had a lot of terrier blood in him, and who knew what else. The pup reminded her of Kevin, strong and resilient, but not intense. After all he'd been through, he was still calm, though when he awoke, he did continue to stare at Abby as though afraid she might disappear. When Abby left the room to change the water in her bucket, the pup rushed after her, sitting at her feet until it was time to return to the other room.

As the day wore on, she thought about names. She'd have to find a name for the little guy that reflected his attributes. She wondered what Kevin would say if she named the puppy after him. That made her smile. But she finally decided against it. It would be too confusing to have two Kevins around; and she hoped she'd still see Kevin once the work on the salon was done.

It was almost time to leave for Aunty Lili's and dinner when Abby finally knew what the dog's name should be. A fine, strong name, one he could be inspired by, a name to live up to. She'd name him Mano—"shark."

Aunty Lili eyed the puppy with trepidation.

"A dog?"

"Kevin and the guys rescued it this morning, along with Greg. They say it's a stray who needs a home, and that he might have been trapped in the gully for a week. See how skinny he is?"

The sight of the poor animal's ribs won Aunty Lili over. She clicked her tongue and hurried into the kitchen for some hamburger she said was getting old and would be good to feed to the dog.

Abby followed behind, trying hard to hide the smile she felt blooming. She'd known Aunty wouldn't be able to resist once she heard the sad story.

As they watched the puppy eat, Abby decided it was time to test Kevin's theory. She hoped her voice remained casual.

"Kevin thought you'd feel more comfortable about me living in town if I had a watchdog."

Aunty seemed to consider it. "It's a good idea."

Then she looked skeptically at the little animal. "But this is a watchdog? He's such a little thing, and so skinny."

Abby already felt an owner's pride in Mano. He wasn't *that* skinny. "Well, Greg thinks he's only a few months old. So I'm sure he'll grow. But even a little dog can be a good watchdog. All they have to do is make a lot of noise and scare people away."

Aunty frowned. "What if he barks at your clients and scares them?"

Abby bit her lip. "I hadn't thought of that. Oh, dear."

This sent her to the phone, using the cell phone number Kevin had given her for the first time. She did remember to ask if he could talk before she began; after all, he was at work.

"I just introduced Mano to Aunty Lili," she began.

"Who?" Kevin said. "What?"

His confusion was obvious, and Abby backpedaled.

"I just got home with that dog."

" 'That dog?' Uh-oh, this doesn't sound good. What did he do? Leave a mess on Aunty Lili's carpet?"

In the background, Abby could hear voices. She didn't know the setup at the firehouse, but it sounded like the others were right there listening in.

"No, nothing like that. But Aunty Lili brought up something you didn't think to mention. If he's going to be a good watchdog, what's to prevent him scaring my clients? Will he bark at them? I've always had cats, so a dog is a new experience. And some people are afraid of dogs."

There was a momentary silence on the other end of the line.

"Are you still there?" Abby asked.

"Yeah. I'm here. I'm thinking."

"That's what that noise was. That squeaky sound, like a rusty wheel."

"Okay, okay." He grumbled at her but she could detect the smile in his voice.

"I've got it. My sister has this gate you put up in a doorway to keep kids from falling down the stairs. People use them for pets too, to keep them in a particular room. You can keep him in the kitchen or bedroom during working hours."

Abby thought this over.

"Are you there?"

This time it was Kevin who asked.

She had to smile. "That was my line."

She looked down at little Mano. He'd finished his ground beef and sat at her feet, staring at her with his big brown eyes. The adoration in his gaze was obvious.

"Okay. I guess I can get a gate." She sighed. Another expense. But she was already attached to Mano; she didn't want to give him back.

"You don't have to get one. My nephews are long past the age where she needs that gate. I'll borrow it for you."

"Thanks."

"No problem."

She bent down to pet Mano, who rewarded her with a few quick laps of her wrist.

"What did you say you named him?"

Abby smiled. "Mano."

There was a moment of silence.

"You called him shark?"

"Yep. I decided he'd had a rough time of it and survived, so he deserved a good strong name. And it gives him something to live up to. He'll have to be strong and fierce like a *mano* if he wants to be a good watchdog."

"Okay." He paused again, as if thinking this over. "If you say so."

Abby thought she heard amusement in his voice, but she couldn't be sure.

Chapter Eight

Mano quickly became Abby's shadow. He followed her everywhere. He whined when she moved out of his sight, and was shy around strangers, though he took to Aunty Lili and would happily spend time with her. So far he hadn't shown any particular talent as a watchdog, but Abby wasn't about to mention that to Aunty Lili. She seemed relieved at the thought of Abby having a dog with her at the salon, and Abby didn't plan to start her fretting again.

Kevin called several times a day to check on the pup's progress. Or so he claimed. At odd times of the day, as she played with her new best friend, Abby would wonder if Kevin could truly be so concerned about Mano's welfare. But since she delighted in their conversations, she didn't question his motives. She decided she loved the attention—of both her men. So she'd just continue to enjoy it.

It also occurred to her that spending so much time with the same men at the station might make Kevin long for the sound of a female voice. He did start each conversation by asking about Mano, but after that their talk would cover a wide range of subjects. They might speak together for a few minutes or for an hour. It depended on his schedule, the emergency calls the station received, and her own sense of whether or not she could spare the time.

She was very busy as the opening of The Hair Place drew near. One week and she'd be moving into the house. Once in, she'd be open for business immediately. She even had a few appointments lined up. Some friends of Aunty Lili's had already arranged for haircuts, and she'd contacted Kevin's generous neighbor and scheduled his daughters, as well.

Proudly, she placed her appointment book on the counter beside the client chair as she organized all of her essential paraphernalia in the drawers underneath.

As she sorted inventory, cleaned, hung posters on the walls, and found inexpensive but attractive area rugs, Abby tried not to think about Kevin. Mano's presence made that difficult, though, as did the fact that just being in the main part of the house brought constant memories of their interaction. How could she forget that they'd been standing just inside the main room when they considered the possibility that

Aunty Lili was matchmaking? And they were working at the opposite end of the room when Kevin told her about his high school baseball career. And of course any foray into the kitchen brought memories of their day painting the walls and ceiling, and of the thick awareness between them that was present that day.

No, keeping her mind away from Kevin was definitely not an easy task.

On his part, Kevin felt like a fool for calling Abby so often. The other guys on his shift were ribbing him unmercifully. His excuse about checking on the dog didn't make them cut him any slack.

Not counting their time in elementary school, he'd only known Abby for about ten days. But they'd spent a lot of time together in those ten days, and he liked to think they'd established a close friendship. He found himself wondering what she was doing while he was at work. Was she still cleaning the house? Had she found the *pareaus* she wanted for covering the sofa and chair? Was she painting the bedroom without him?

Memories of their morning painting the kitchen had a strange effect on him. The day had been dark and humid, the room small and close. But he couldn't stop thinking about the time they'd spent there, the way their shoulders would brush as they moved from paint tray to wall, the sound of her voice as she told him about her plans. He'd succumbed to temptation and kissed her good-night that one time. How he'd wanted to do it again, right there in the kitchen with the air heavy with moisture and saturated with the smell of wet paint. And even then, he could detect the suggestion of jasmine that always seemed to surround her.

He couldn't lose the memory of that first kiss, didn't want to. It had been wonderful, her lips sweeter than he'd dared to hope. Maybe if he kissed her again, it would help assuage the desire, and he could stop thinking about it whenever he was with her.

But he was trying to step back and away. She was Aunty Lili's niece and godchild, under her protection, even if she was over twenty-one. Also, he didn't want to endanger their fragile new friendship. It was built on common interests and mutual respect. He liked spending time with her, and wanted to keep on doing it.

So asking after Mano was as good an excuse as any to call and talk. Just hearing her voice gave him a pleasure he tried to keep from the other guys.

And he wasn't pretending a concern for Mano. The little dog had affected him in an unexpected manner. He'd been in on such rescues before, but there was something about the spirit of this particular animal that spoke to him. He would have adopted him in an instant if he could. But his job and his odd schedule precluded having any pets. His mother and teenage sister had two cats who were too old to accept a young dog into the house. His older sister already had both a dog and a cat. And while his two nephews would love the new addition, she would probably kill him for bringing them another animal.

Then he'd remembered Abby. She was a natural for the little guy. She was a hard worker, but she was also a nurturer. He'd seen that in her treatment of the women at the care center. And his inspiration about her having a watchdog was the clincher.

"Are you on the phone with your girlfriend again?"

Jim's joking voice pulled him out of a brief reverie after he hung up the phone.

"She's not my girlfriend."

"Sure." Jim slapped him on the back. "That's why you spend so much time helping her out and talking to her."

"When is she going to fix that sorry haircut of yours?" Dave asked.

Gil was now officially on leave, taking time to spend with his new family, and Kevin missed him already. Dave was his cousin on his father's side, and the two of had been competitive since childhood. They were also such different personality types that they grated on each other. Kevin often thought it was a real shame Dave had also become a firefighter, throwing them together at work as well as at family events.

"What's wrong with my haircut?"

"Nothing. If you were a shaggy dog. And it's too

long," he added. "Now that you're such friends, she might like to fix you up. You know, for free." He grinned. "Maybe it'll help improve that ugly mug of yours."

Kevin just shrugged off his cousin's words. He knew there was nothing wrong with his looks. He never had any trouble finding a date, but he didn't want to get into a bragging match with Dave.

"You're just jealous that I've got a good thick head of hair and your forehead is getting higher."

Dave's face immediately clouded. His hairline was a touchy subject.

"Boys, boys," Jim said. "Come on. Time to start the chili."

As they moved into the kitchen and began to ready their meal, Kevin made one more attempt to explain.

"Abby's been pretty busy working on the house. And now she's got that dog we dropped on her. I just want to make sure she can handle him okay."

"You're such a humanitarian." Dave's comment dripped with sarcasm.

Before any more could be said, their alarm rang. *So much for dinner*, Kevin thought.

Between caring for Mano and Kevin's phone calls, Abby found she wasn't getting as much accomplished. But she didn't think she cared. The time spent on the phone with Kevin, Mano sleeping warmly in her lap, made her feel good.

So she was surprised at the irritation that flooded her voice when she picked up the phone on Friday evening and heard Kevin's voice—again.

"Mano's fine," she said, then instantly regretted the tone of her voice. "Sorry." She found herself apologizing before he took offense. She valued their new friendship, and hoped it would continue. "You got me in the middle of doing my nails, and I got some polish on the receiver."

Kevin apologized in his turn.

"I'm not calling to check on Mano. This is something personal."

Fascinated, Abby forgot her smudged nail, turning her full attention to the person at the other end of the line. "Personal?"

"I need a favor."

"Okay." She was practically spellbound now. Kevin was much more closemouthed about himself than she was. He'd learned her life story while they worked together at The Hair Place, but she knew only bits and pieces about his personal side.

She was sure he was smiling when he replied. She could hear it in his voice.

"Don't you want to know what the favor is before you agree?"

"Sure. But I doubt it'll be anything illegal, so I'll help you out. After all you've done for me, it's the least I can do."

His voice sobered. "That's not why I did it, you know. So that you'd be indebted, I mean."

"I know." Tenderness for his freely-offered friendship spread a warmth through her chest. "So what did you want? A great haircut before your big weekend date? Some highlights?"

There was a short pause.

"Highlights? You're kidding, right?"

Abby laughed. "I am. But lots of guys get highlights. It's just that you already have natural ones, so you don't need any."

There was another short pause before Kevin said anything more. When he did, he changed the subject completely.

"Look, I know your place isn't ready yet, but you could do someone's hair there, couldn't you?"

Abby hesitated. Was this the "personal" favor? Curiosity was killing her. He hadn't taken her up on her offer of a haircut a moment ago. Just what did he want that he was calling a personal favor?

"Yeah. The place isn't all fixed up, but I could do someone's hair. I'm ready to go."

"Good." There was another pause. "I really need a favor for my sister."

Ahhh, now he was getting to it.

"The one who lent me the gate?" she asked.

"No, my younger sister. She's still in high school."

"Wow. I didn't know you had a sister that young."

How had she not known that? Aunty Lili had talked about Kevin on and off since she'd arrived in Malino, and she'd never mentioned a teenaged sister. Abby could picture Kevin spoiling a sister so much his junior.

But the smile this conjured up faded quickly when he began to explain the problem.

"The high school prom is coming up," he began.

"Yeah, I know. I planned my opening to catch prom season and the June weddings."

"Somehow, I'm not surprised to hear that," Kevin said. "People look at your mod hairstyle and all those earrings and think you're young and flaky. But there's a hardworking and astute businesswoman under those purple streaks."

Abby's throat felt tight at his compliment. "Thank you. That's the nicest thing anyone's ever said to me."

"You don't know the right people," he muttered, but Abby heard every word. It almost brought a tear to her eye. It did put a lump in her throat.

"Well." He cleared his throat, as though the lump was mutual. "The thing is, Ramona thought she'd give herself some red highlights. She said something about a concert she was at last month, and the singer's hair," he explained. "Anyway, she tried to give her hair some red streaks, and it was a disaster. She's crying her eyes out, and Mom is beside herself. Do you think you can do something to help?"

"Oh, the poor thing. Of course I can help. I have

most of my supplies already, and I've been stocking the cutting station. Can they meet me at The Hair Place?"

"I'll tell them." Kevin's voice softened, and Abby felt little tingles along her nape at the delicious sound of his thank you. "*Mahalo*, Abby."

Twenty minutes later, Abby was peering out the front windows at The Hair Place. Mano danced about at her feet, agitated, as if he sensed that something different was afoot.

Finally, she saw a white sedan pull up. An attractive woman of about fifty who must have been Mrs. Palea got out, along with someone wearing an old straw hat, jeans and a large T-shirt. Abby assumed it was Kevin's sister, though the age and sex of the person was indeterminable from her view. The brim of the straw hat was pulled down so low, her face couldn't be seen at all. Her mother's hat, Abby would bet. Probably used for gardening. She'd also bet that under ordinary circumstances, the teenager wouldn't be caught dead wearing it.

Abby hurried forward, opening the door for them. Only the younger girl's chin showed as she walked forward, and Abby wondered how she could see to maneuver up the steps. But she managed to make it through the door unscathed. Abby noticed that Mano hung back, a bit shy with the strangers. She'd already discerned that open doors were not a problem with him. He never ran out, only followed her when she walked outside. Apparently, he'd had more than enough of freedom.

"Thank you so much for offering to help," Mrs. Palea said. "I'm Rebecca. I've heard all about you from Aunty Liliuokalani and Kevin," she added. "I'm so glad you've come back to Malino."

She turned to the figure at her side. "And this is Ramona. We really appreciate you making time for us."

"No problem," Abby assured them. She shook hands with Rebecca and invited Ramona to remove her hat and sit in the styling chair. Instead of complying, the young girl burst into tears and gestured toward the wide windows and the Dairy Queen across the street. On a Friday night, the tables there overflowed with teenagers.

"I *can't*," she wailed.

Mano stepped around Abby's legs, cocking his head as he peered up at the sobbing girl.

"Oh. Sorry," Abby said.

Instantly, Abby realized she should have lowered the bamboo shades all the way before her first client arrived, but she'd been so preoccupied with what the young girl must be going through, she hadn't thought of it. Even with concern for the teen uppermost in her mind, though, Abby couldn't help the little thrill that passed through her as she thought in terms of her *first* client.

Abby stepped up to the window and lowered the

shade closest to the work station, and Rebecca helped with the rest. Mano, Abby noticed, remained near Ramona, still looking at her curiously.

"You've done wonders with this old place," Rebecca commented. "It looks real good."

"Thanks," Abby said, placing a comforting hand on Ramona's arm and guiding her into the chair.

"Aunty Liliuokalani said I absolutely could not live here unless I covered those windows, but I hadn't thought about how useful the shades would be at a time like this. I think Aunty Lili imagines me walking around in my underwear or something. And since I had Kevin widen the doors into what used to be the living room, she figures I'll need to close these every night. I haven't decided yet," she finished, reaching for the straw hat and tipping it up enough to see Ramona's tear ravaged face. "But it's good to know I can close the place up for emergencies. These things do happen, you know."

Ramona darted a quick look toward the street, assuring herself the windows were indeed covered. Then she glanced at the room itself, and finally at Abby.

"It's really different," she said. "It's nice."

"Thank you." Abby stood beside her, allowing time for her to calm down and relax.

"I used to get my hair done here when I was a kid," Ramona said.

Abby hid a smile. As though she was so old now.

But then, back when she was sixteen or seventeen, she probably felt that her "kid" days were long behind her too.

"It was kind of gloomy in here then. Patty was pretty nice, though," Ramona said. "She used to always wear pink. She matched the walls, you know?"

Abby laughed. "I'd forgotten that, but my friend Julie said the same thing about her clothes."

Abby could see that Ramona was feeling better. With a deep breath, she reached up for the hat. At the last minute, though, her courage deserted her. She stopped, hands stilled on the brim of the old straw hat as a sob caught in her throat. Mano, his canine intuition working at warp speed, immediately put his head in her lap and focused his large eyes on her face.

"I did some weird things with my hair when I was a teenager," Abby told Ramona. "Had a few disasters too."

Abby remembered laughing hysterically a few times at the results of her experiments, but she'd never cried like this. However, in L.A., looking outrageous was not a problem. Things were different in a small town like Malino. And of course, this was the prom. Perfect hair was a necessity.

"Come on. You have to let me see, or I won't be able to help." She used her warmest voice, coaxing the teen as she had her pet cat when he would sneak into the narrow space behind the refrigerator.

With perfect timing, Mano placed his paws on her lap and whined, and Ramona finally lifted her arms. The hat went into the air, falling behind her onto the floor. Her eyes closed as her hair tumbled out and she grasped Mano's forelegs and drew him onto her lap. She hugged the little dog close as her hair fanned over her shoulders and brushed her shoulder blades. She took one peek in the mirror and began to sob anew.

Oh, dear, Abby thought, viewing the bright orange streaks for the first time. A red that was all wrong for her coloring, probably with peroxide in it, and left on the hair for far too long.

Out loud she said, "No problem," just as Mano whined again. Ramona was probably squeezing him too tightly, but Abby silently thanked him for the distraction.

Ramona swiped at her tears, then turned her attention to the dog.

"This is Mano," Abby said. "Did Kevin tell you about how the guys rescued him?"

She told them how the little dog had looked when Kevin brought him over, and how she'd cleaned him up and fed him. And she told them how she'd chosen a strong name for him, giving him something to be proud of, to live up to.

All the while, she examined Ramona's hair. She put her hands into it, spreading the damaged strands out so that she could examine them. The hair was over-treated and dry, and felt more like straw than hair. Still, she had every confidence that she would be able to restore it.

She smiled confidently into Ramona's face in the mirror. She noticed that the girl clung to Mano, clutching him close like a toddler might a favorite stuffed toy.

"I can fix it for you. The color will be easy. And a hot moisturizing treatment will help the dryness."

The relief that flooded Ramona's face brought a warm feeling to Abby's chest. *There's nothing like helping someone fix a problem,* Abby thought. It was almost as good as arranging the hair of the ladies at the care center. She couldn't wait to see Ramona's reaction when they were done and she got a look at her restored hair. It still gave her pleasure to think of how happy all the elderly ladies at the care home had been with their stylings.

"Kevin said you were trying for highlights. While I'm fixing up the color, I can give you some. What do you think?"

Ramona looked from her mother to Abby and back again.

"Could you really?" Her voice was thin but hopeful.

"Fix your hair?" Abby said. "Sure. No problem. And highlights? Piece of cake." She suppressed an urge to grin, deciding that a serious, businesslike demeanor was more appropriate in this instance. "First we'll repigment, to get you back to your natural color. Then I'll put in some nice caramel highlights. You don't want to go too light or too red with your dark hair. But think of the color of hot caramel drizzling over vanilla ice cream. It will be beautiful."

Ramona hiccupped and fixed a look of sheer adoration on Abby as she passed into the shampoo room, seeking the proper colors to mix for the job ahead. Mano, relishing the attention from Ramona, lapped at her chin. Abby was delighted when the girl giggled at the action.

Rebecca nodded to Abby and headed for the seating area. As she mixed the hair color, Abby saw Rebecca pull a paperback romance novel from her purse and settle back into the sofa.

"So, I hear the prom is coming up," Abby said as she began daubing color on Ramona's damaged hair. The sooner she covered those orange stripes the better, she thought, moving her brush rapidly along the first part she'd made in the young girl's hair. "What's your dress like?"

It was a subject close to any teenage girl's heart, and sure enough Ramona began to talk. By the time Abby had finished applying the dark dye, Ramona had some color in her cheeks, and the bleak look was gone from her eyes. Abby hoped she felt better too.

"We'll have to wait now for the color to set," Abby told her. "Usually I have another client to work on while you sit and look at magazines or whatever. But today it's just us, so what do you say we go inside and

look through my video collection? See what we can
find."

Some of her original reticence returned as Ramona
rose from the chair and followed Abby inside. Mano
remained close, apparently adopting Ramona as his
special friend for the duration. A glimmer of interest
flickered across her tear-stained face when Abby
pulled out a box filled with videos.

Ramona lowered herself to the floor beside the carton, pulling a willing Mano into her lap. "You don't
have DVDs?"

Abby laughed, and she noticed Rebecca smile.
"Most of these go back to when I was your age, so,
no, there aren't any DVDs. But, hey, these are classics." Although Rebecca was twice her age, they
exchanged an understanding look at the expression
on the younger girl's face.

Abby reached into the box and pulled out a couple
of tapes. "I was living in L.A. and into movies, so
I've got a lot of the old classics. Ever seen
Casablanca?"

"I don't think so," Ramona said, looking at the
black-and-white still on the front of the tape box.

"Oh, what a great movie that is," Rebecca said,
putting her finger into her book to hold her place. "So
romantic." She sighed.

Abby saw Ramona widen her eyes in surprise at her
mother's comment. "Let's put it on," Abby suggested.
"Everyone should see *Casablanca* at least once."

Ramona didn't object. She started to sit on the sofa beside her mother.

"Wait!" Rebecca stopped her before she could lower herself to the cushion. "You might get hair dye on the sofa. Better sit on the wooden chair."

Abby almost held her breath, wondering what the teen's reaction would be. She hated to tell a client where she had to sit, but she did hope to use this furniture for a while, and it was already old.

"Sorry, I should have realized," Ramona said. She looked over to Abby. "Is it okay if I bring this chair closer?" She gestured to one of the brightly painted chairs Abby had situated near the new doorway.

"Sure. Pull it up. I'm going to get some *pareaus* to cover the sofa, but I don't have the place quite finished yet."

"*Pareaus?*" Ramona said. "That will be colorful."

Abby wasn't sure whether or not the teenager thought it was a good idea or not, but she didn't let it bother her. It was her place, her dream.

"It's going to be awhile, so I think I'll put some popcorn in the microwave." She didn't have much in the way of food in the house yet, but she had purchased a microwave and brought in some tea bags, snack food, and dog food. "Be right back."

Mano, always alert to a trip into the kitchen, jumped off Ramona's lap and hurried after Abby.

* * *

Her first client experience became fun—a kind of tri-generational slumber party. Except that they weren't going to sleep there.

The movie was a hit. They stopped it when it was time to rinse out the dye, then restarted it once Abby had finished applying the new dye and the foil strips for the highlights. At the end of the movie, Ramona cried along with her mother and Abby.

"That was wonderful," she said, dabbing at her damp cheeks with a tissue. This latest bout of crying was of a gentler nature than what she'd been doing when she arrived. This was the kind of crying that made you feel good.

"It's always been one of my favorites," Rebecca said.

The three of them discussed movies while Abby continued with Ramona's hair. Rebecca's book lay forgotten on the coffee table.

Once Abby rinsed out the highlight color and shampooed Ramona's hair, she applied a conditioner and put the teen under the dryer for ten minutes. And they continued to talk.

It wasn't until Abby was finished, and smiling as widely as Ramona at her beautiful dark hair, that she asked about her hairstyle for the prom.

"So, how will you be wearing your hair?"

"I wasn't sure. I was going to try some things tomorrow with a friend."

"I can show you a few styles," Abby said. "If you'd like," she added.

"Oh, I would. Thank you," Ramona said. "That would be so great."

"Maybe we could make an appointment to have Abby do your hair," Rebecca suggested. Ramona was delighted, as was Abby. She practically skipped over to her appointment book and grinned as she found the date and entered the time.

"You're my first appointment for that day, so you get your choice of times," Abby said. "And don't forget to bring a photo of your gown."

"I won't."

By the time Abby had done a few sample dos for Ramona, it was after midnight. The three women were still wide awake and "talking story," acting like old friends. They didn't even hear the car pull up outside. Or see Mano dash across the room and stand waiting beside the door.

"You left the door unlocked again," Kevin announced, walking inside the salon and closing the door behind him. Then he made a point of turning around and locking it. After that, he took a moment to greet the exuberant Mano.

Abby, staring at him across the long room, couldn't hide her surprise, or her pleasure. She was delighted that Kevin could now see how nice his sister's hair looked.

His reaction was everything she'd hoped.

Kevin was stunned. He hadn't seen Ramona's hair, but he'd heard about the screaming orange from his mother. She'd sounded almost as upset as Ramona when she first called him.

Now he saw three beaming women. One of them did have strange hair, but that was Abby, with her spiked, purple-tipped locks. That matched her purple nails. Beside her was Ramona, her hair falling past her shoulders, wavy and beautiful. The streaks reminded him of candy—the golden strips of caramel that trailed from a candy bar after your first bite.

"Wow."

Ramona smiled shyly, proud of her brother's reaction. Abby beamed. His mother smiled quietly, her eyes radiating happiness.

"Nice, huh?" Ramona said. She put one hand up to her hair, letting her fingers run through the ends.

"It's a miracle," Rebecca said.

Abby smiled, obviously pleased with her clients' reactions.

"What are you doing here?" Abby asked Kevin. "Not that it's not nice to see you, but it is late. And we were having girls' night out here."

"Okay. I know when I'm not wanted."

However, he didn't make a move to leave. Instead, he looked over at his mother.

"What do you think of the work Abby's done in here?"

"I told her how nice it is. She did a good job."

"Kevin did a lot," Abby mentioned.

But Kevin brushed off her attempt at being humble. "You planned it all, I just helped with implementation."

"Are you off work now?" Abby asked.

Changing the subject, he thought with a grin. He answered with a nod. He was off and there were things he could be doing. But he'd been irresistibly drawn to The Hair Place. He tried to persuade himself it was because of Ramona. But he knew he was just fooling himself.

Abruptly, he decided he should go.

"Okay. I can see you women don't want a man around." He tweaked Ramona on the chin. "You look terrific, kid."

He headed for the door. "Lock up behind me," he called over his shoulder.

Abby made a face at his back, and Ramona giggled.

"We should be going too," Rebecca said. She reached for her wallet. "What do we owe you?"

"Don't be silly." Abby looked offended. "Kevin has done so much for me. He asked for a favor, and that's what I did. I was happy to oblige."

But Rebecca was firm. "This is your business. You had to use supplies that cost you money. So I insist."

She pushed a folded bill into Abby's hand, and

Abby decided not to argue. She might be an artist with hair, but she was practical, especially when it came to business matters.

She hugged Rebecca. "Don't be strangers. Come over anytime; you don't have to be getting your hair done."

She turned to Ramona, giving her a hug too.

"And Ramona is going to tell all her friends about The Hair Place, giving me a ton of free advertising, right, Ramona?" Abby said with a grin.

"Oh, yes. I'm sure other people will want to get highlights when they see my hair." She touched her newly done hair, obviously relishing the feel of the moisturized tresses. "I'll warn my friends not to try doing it themselves."

"Amen," Rebecca and Abby murmured.

Chapter Nine

"I've got a surprise for you."

Kevin was back at The Hair Place the next morning, though Abby hadn't expected him. The main work on the salon was done; what remained were the decorative touches she'd have to handle herself.

"A surprise? Really?"

Abby's smile was spontaneous and wide. She looked just as happy to see him as Mano did.

"What is it?"

Her eager voice made his grin even wider. He especially liked the way her eyes lit up. Her reaction reminded him of his nephews' excitement over new toys. Too many grownups lost that easy pleasure in the simple things.

"Come on out here. I have it in the truck."

They walked outside together, Mano trailing behind. The sun was high in the sky, the light outside bright enough to hurt the eyes. Kevin pulled out his sunglasses, tucked handily into his T-shirt neckline. Abby, not so conveniently equipped, blinked and squinted.

"It's not another dog, is it?"

She looked down at Mano, standing calmly beside them, his eyes always alert to Abby's whereabouts and activities.

"Nope. One dog is plenty. Though I'm not sure Mano is going to work out as a watchdog." He raised a skeptical brow at the animal, who wagged his tail happily at the attention.

"Ramona really liked him," Abby said. "How come you didn't take him over to her?"

He shook his head as he bent to pet the friendly mutt. "I really did think he'd work out as a watchdog. And Ma and Ramona have two old cats. I don't think they'd welcome a puppy into the house. The cats, I mean, not Ma and Ramona."

"Oh." Abby had to admit that made sense. Older animals just wanted to live out their lives in peace, and puppies always wanted to play.

That settled, her gaze moved over to Kevin's Durango.

"So, what's my surprise?" Abby asked.

Kevin straightened up, dusting his hands off, even

though Abby knew Mano's fur was clean. Just one of those gestures men made, she supposed.

As Kevin opened up the rear of the Durango, Abby leaned forward in anticipation. She looked into the truck, then turned her gaze back to Kevin. The eager expectation had turned to doubt.

"Uh. It's paint."

Uh-oh. She was surprised, all right. But suddenly he was uncertain about his gift. He'd thought she'd be happy, as she'd certainly been at the suggestion of something special. He'd felt sure she'd be delighted by his present. Had he figured this wrong?

Oh, well. Too late to back out now.

"Come on."

Kevin took a gallon in each hand and gestured her toward the kitchen door. She closed the back of the truck and followed him inside, still appearing uncertain and wary. Mano, on the other hand, trotted happily back into the house.

"I heard you had a birthday just before you arrived in Malino," Kevin said, entering the kitchen and depositing his paint on the counter. "So I thought I'd bring over a late gift. Ma contributed too, as a thank-you for last night."

"Okay." Abby finally smiled. "Though your Mom insisted on paying for the dye and conditioner."

She looked from the paint cans to him again, a gleam lighting her eyes. "Hmm. You heard I had a birthday, huh? I suppose a little bird told you—a tall and thin senior citizen bird, maybe?"

"I'm not telling." He took a screwdriver from his back pocket and applied it to the top of the can. "There have to be a few secrets among friends, you know. To make things interesting."

He continued to work at the can lid as he spoke.

"Anyway, I know you've been too busy to get around to buying paint for the bedroom. I checked with Aunty Lili and Julie. And since I figure I'm the reason for that, I thought I'd help you out."

"You're the reason?" Abby was still confused.

Kevin nodded. "Mano. He's been taking up a lot of your time."

He noticed that she didn't argue with him over that. He stifled a sigh. He'd hoped the pup would help her relax, but he might have inadvertently made her life even busier.

"So, I figured if I hadn't dropped Mano on you, you'd probably have repainted the bedroom by now."

"You bought paint for the bedroom?"

"I saw the color of the room back there, and it's definitely not you."

Abby worked to keep her facial expression impassive. She agreed that the color wasn't her. She'd never been a pink person. And she did mean to repaint it. But it wasn't that important; as long as the salon was ready, it could wait. At least the color in the room was light, not the dark shade of the old salon.

But Kevin had chosen a color for her? Should she be apprehensive?

"Don't get nervous. You're going to love it."

Did he wink at her?

Although she was thrilled that he'd thought to surprise her with such a practical gift, she couldn't help noticing how he seemed almost able to read her mind. Just how *did* he know she was a nervous wreck wondering what color he'd chosen for her bedroom?

Abby clasped her hands tightly together.

"Okay. Let's see it."

She thought her voice remained nicely calm. She tried to smile.

Oh, dear. What if it was purple? If he'd decided lavender was her color, would she be able to smile and say "wonderful"? He was always associating her with the color purple, and she did love it. Just not on walls.

"This will be just like the famous reveals on those home improvement shows on TV," he said.

He looked so excited, Abby's concern receded enough for her to feel some of that initial delight. Mano, catching their mood, leaped around on the floor at their feet, jumping up as though he too was eager to see the color.

Abby prepared to show her happiness with the paint, no matter what color it was. How could she feel bad about it, when he was so happy? It was a sweet gesture, and she appreciated it more than if he'd arrived with a dozen roses.

She held her breath.

Then the paint lid was off, and she breathed a sigh of relief. She wouldn't have to pretend.

"It's great! It's wonderful!"

The paint was a shade of blue-green that reminded her of the clearest part of the ocean. It was a color she could get lost in when she retreated to her own room at the end of the day. She'd have a cool oasis of a room for her private moments.

"I love it. It's like looking out the plane window and seeing how clear and beautiful the water is . . . It's wonderful."

"I knew you'd like it. It's called 'Pacific Shallows.' Of course, Julie did tell me that you looked at something like this when you two went shopping." He felt proud of his initiative in consulting with her best friend. "If we start right away, we can get it done before lunch."

Impulsively, Abby hugged Kevin, giving him a kiss on the cheek. Unfortunately, he was leaning against the counter, his weight supported on one leg, so that she knocked him off balance. He put his arms around her, trying to recover, but it didn't help. The two of them tumbled to the floor in a tangle of arms and legs. Mano yipped as they landed, apparently catching one of his paws beneath them.

"Oh, my gosh, is Mano okay? We didn't tip the paint can over, did we?"

Concern about spilling paint all over her newly done kitchen couldn't stop her from laughing, though, as Mano's head appeared between them. He lapped at each face alternately, until they pushed the excited pup away.

"I think Mano is fine." Kevin's dry voice came from somewhere near her left ear.

Abby was breathless when she finally managed to raise herself up off the floor. She checked the counter.

"Whew. Everything's fine," she said. "I'm sure glad we didn't knock that can over on the way down." She turned to Kevin. "I like my present. I wouldn't want to lose it."

Kevin took his time getting to his feet. He was breathless too, but not because of laughter over Mano's antics. No, he had a lump the size of Lanai caught in his throat for a completely different reason.

He took a minute to brush off his clothing—not because it was dusty, but because he needed the time to reorganize. He could still feel the imprint of Abby's body against him, her soft curves pressing against his hard muscle. . .

He took a deep breath and straightened up. She looked so thin, you'd expect her to feel sharp and bony. Instead, she was soft in all the right places, and he was paying the price right now.

He cleared his throat.

"You still have all the painting stuff, don't you?"

Abby didn't seem at all fazed by their recent tumble. She was almost bouncing as she looked again into the can of paint.

"Are you kidding? With Aunty Lili as a major influence in my life? Of course, I kept all that stuff. It's in the storage area under the house." Like many old homes constructed in the plantation style, the house was built up off the ground, with a crawl space some three feet high underneath, closed off with wooden rails. A gate near the back door provided access to the storage area, which worked well for lawn equipment and other detritus of home life.

Kevin went out to get the things, and Abby headed for the bedroom.

"I'll start putting the furniture into a pile," she said.

Kevin took off his light jacket and threw it over the back of a kitchen chair before he went outside. It was feeling darned warm in the kitchen at the moment, and he didn't think the bedroom would be much better. No, the room was small, so he'd be close to Abby the entire time they worked. Man, he wished she hadn't tripped and fallen into him that way!

Memories of her body seemed imprinted on his. He could still feel the soft indent where her hip had pressed into his belly, the . . .

For gosh sakes, he scolded himself, *don't think about it!*

He saw the cardboard box labeled "paint things"

and pulled it out. It was a cool morning, with a misty rain dampening the air. He tossed his head back, drinking in the freshness of it. Unfortunately, it would take more than the island's famous "liquid sunshine" to cool him off this morning.

Abby was done with the furniture when Kevin returned to the room. She'd opened all the windows for ventilation, and she couldn't tell if the wonderful fragrance came from outside or from Kevin himself. Because as soon as he walked into the room, she could smell the fresh, moist air with its briny tinge of the ocean. There was another, earthier aroma that came with it, like freshly turned soil in a garden.

She couldn't help noting the muscles rippling along his arms as he lifted the box away from Mano's curious nose.

"Good thing I brought that gate with me. I think we're going to need it."

Abby had to agree. Painting with a curious puppy in the room would be a recipe for disaster.

As her gaze moved from Mano to Kevin, she found her body temperature increasing. Kevin looked his usual handsome self. But there was moisture on his skin, beading along his arms and in his hair. It brought attention to his fine arms and the muscles that rippled beneath his brown skin.

And his hair! Of course, she was partial to hair, and

his was especially fine and healthy. Those raindrops sparkling on it made her want to plunge her hands into the thick strands. She really would love to style his hair. She'd have to see if she could talk him into it.

"Ah . . ." Abby stammered as she momentarily forgot what she'd meant to say. Way too many distractions this morning.

Oh, yes, the painting.

"It's ready for the taping," she said. "I have the masking tape in a drawer in the kitchen."

She hurried to get it, forgetting that she'd have to slide past Kevin to get out the door. The bedroom was small, and with the bed and dressers pushed into the center of the room, there was little space for movement along the sides. As she passed by Kevin, their bodies brushed, her arm collecting some dampness from the raindrops that remained on his skin. She felt the hairs on her arm stand up, alert to the delicious feeling of his cool skin against hers. She remembered how warm he'd been just minutes ago when they'd tumbled to the floor.

She stopped, embarrassed and uncertain of how to proceed. Finally, she murmured, "I'll be right back," and scurried from the room.

Kevin watched her leave, a small smile playing at his lips. He'd gotten what felt like an electric shock when she'd slid against him just now. It wasn't, of course; there was way too much moisture in the air for any kind of a static charge.

Abby was not unaffected; he could see it in the way she averted her eyes, and hung her head as she rushed out the door. *Well, well.* It looked like the morning might be a repeat of Tuesday in the kitchen. Another cold shower tonight.

Remembering only too well the tension associated with their working together in the kitchen, Abby watched Kevin begin on the far wall and moved to the one opposite. Just being together in the bedroom was suggestive; she didn't want to keep literally bumping into him. He always smelled so good too. She wished she could ask him about it, but she was fairly certain it wasn't cologne. That, you could ask about. *Gee, that's a nice cologne you're wearing, what's it called?* But how did you ask a man what kind of soap he used without sounding like a complete idiot?

Abby dipped her roller into the tray and continued rolling out her wall. The blue-green color was as lovely as she'd imagined. Already, she could feel how soothing it would be to come in here and relax after a busy day.

Kevin was quiet this morning, and she wondered what he was thinking. She was trying to come up with a suitable topic of conversation when Mano suddenly sprang up from the floor on the other side of the gate. He ran across the kitchen, barking all the while. In between, he proffered a few growls.

Shocked to the tips of her toes, Abby stood rooted to the spot, looking after Mano, then toward Kevin.

"What do you suppose he hears?"

As she asked the question, they heard a heavy knocking at the front of the house.

"I guess you finally remembered to lock the door, huh?" Kevin asked. He put his roller in the tray and moved toward the door, stepping over the gate in one smooth movement.

Abby followed, though she doubted her progress over the gate was half as graceful. It would take more practice on her part to negotiate the gate without landing flat on her face. It must be his longer legs.

When Kevin pushed open the kitchen door, Mano broke through, running full tilt into the sitting room and toward the front. There he stood in the inner doorway, feet planted wide apart, his whole body vibrating with the force of his bark.

"Mano. Hush," Abby told him. He stopped momentarily, looking back at her, then moving to stand at her feet. Slightly behind her legs, she noticed. So much for the brave watchdog. His ears stood up. He was still on alert, just cautiously staying behind his mistress.

"It's Greg," Kevin said, opening up the door as he said it.

"Hey. I see the puppy's working out as a watch-dog," Greg said, striding inside and offering his hand to Abby. "Greg Yamamoto. From the animal clinic. I thought I'd check on the little guy."

Now that Greg was inside, and talking in a friendly manner to Abby and Kevin, Mano decided he was okay. At any rate, he stopped barking and even ventured a few tail wags.

"It's nice to meet you. Thanks for the supplies. They were a real life-saver. And as you can see, Mano is doing great." She bent down to lift the dog into her arms, rubbing her head against his as she cuddled him against her. "This is the first time he's acted anything like a watchdog, though. Usually, he just hangs back with me and observes. Then, when he sees I'm okay with whoever it is, he comes out and says hello."

Greg was looking around the room. "The place looks good. Kim will want to come over for a haircut once you're up and running."

"How's married life?" Kevin asked. To Abby's disgust, he gave one of those chuckles men used when talking among themselves about the married state.

"It's good. You should try it."

There was a bit of back-slapping and male bonding, which Abby tried to ignore. Then the three of them went for a tour of the house. Greg apologized when he realized they were in the middle of painting.

"I was just passing by and thought I'd check up on the little guy. What did you call him?"

"Mano." Abby grinned.

Greg looked toward Kevin. "Mano? She named him shark?"

Kevin's answering grin made Abby feel left out—like the guys were bonding again.

"That's what I said, when she told me."

"It's a good strong name for a strong little dog. It also gives him something to be proud of," Abby explained. Again.

That evening, Abby called her mother to tell her about her gift from the Paleas. Unusual as two gallons of paint might be as a birthday surprise, she got a frisson of pleasure every time she thought of her pretty new room. It happened again as she pressed the speed dial button on her cell phone.

"Mom. It's not too late to call, is it?"

She could hear the smile in her mother's voice. "I always have time for my daughter. Nothing's wrong, is it?"

"Oh, no. In fact, things are going well. I had my first client last night."

"I didn't think you were open yet," her mother said. "Did you do Aunty Lili's hair?"

"No. It turns out Kevin has a sister in high school. She was trying to give herself red highlights and turned her hair orange. It was pretty awful."

She could hear her mother click her tongue, and a wave of homesickness for her family filled her.

"I'm sure you took good care of her," Gabrielle said.

"I did. Her mother brought her over, and the three of us had a great time. We watched *Casablanca* and talked about old movies and music. It was a lot of fun."

"That's Rebecca, isn't it?" Gabrielle asked.

"Yes. I take it you know her."

"We were in school together. She's two years older than I am, but I remember her. Her mother always made her beautiful clothing."

"I'd heard that Marian was a great seamstress. I don't think she sews any more, though."

For a few minutes, they spoke about the tragedy of Alzheimer's and the toll it took on families.

Then Abby shared her news. "I had the nicest gift today—a late birthday gift."

She went on to tell her mother about Kevin's surprise, and how he'd been aided and abetted by his mother and Julie. And how the two of them had spent the morning painting her bedroom.

"It looks so great, Mom. It's like sitting under the ocean, the color is so cool and beautiful." A feeling of peace blanketed her as she recalled the new look of the bedroom.

"So now the whole house is redone and ready," she concluded. "I can move in any time, but I'll listen to Aunty Lili and wait until the day before I open up for business. She'll worry about me being there alone, though Mano proved he's a good watchdog this morning." She told her mother how he'd reacted to Greg's surprise visit.

"I'm glad you're enjoying the dog so much. And your room sounds lovely. That Kevin is a special one, Abby. Are you sure you don't want to date him?"

Abby had to laugh at the hope in her mother's voice. "I told you before, Mom. He hasn't asked."

"Aha! So if he did, you would."

Abby shook her head over her mother's assumption, but she was ambivalent. She really hadn't planned to date when she'd arrived in Malino. She had too much to do, and a heavy work schedule. And she was still too hurt by Jack's betrayal. But now that she was past the major hurdles of the renovation, she realized that a date wouldn't be such a horrible thing. As long as the "datee" was Kevin.

When she didn't answer, she heard her mother's soft laughter. "I still think you wouldn't mind. Sometimes you have to admit when you're wrong, you know."

"I know. I admitted I was wrong about Jack, didn't I?"

"That was easy. Your father and I never cared for Jack, you know. But Kevin sounds like a good one. Aunty Lili likes him, and she can usually tell if someone is worth knowing. I wish I could meet him."

Abby wished her mother could meet him too. That would mean having her close, and even though she'd only been gone for two weeks, Abby missed her.

"How's Mano?"

Abby looked at the little terrier mix, snuggled against her side.

"He's well. Curled up right here beside me," she said, dropping her voice. "But don't tell Aunty Lili. She doesn't want him on the furniture, and especially not on the bed." She rubbed Mano's head, scratching the soft fur behind his ears. He turned so that his chin rested on her thigh, and peered up at her through half-closed eyes. Abby thought she might die from the sweet adoration in that gaze.

"I've decided I like having a dog. It's so different from a cat. He follows me around like the most fervent groupie. It's cute."

"And does he like Kevin?"

"He adores him. After all, Kevin rescued him." Abby continued to pet Mano, who rolled over enough to allow for a belly rub.

"Hmm. I do believe in that theory, you know, that you can tell a lot about a man by the way he treats animals. And by the way the animals react to him."

"Well, Kevin is good with teenagers, grandmothers, and dogs." *I don't know how he is with girlfriends, though*, she thought. And she was still a little afraid to find out.

But since she'd spoken the truth to her mother, and Kevin had never asked her out, she doubted there was any chance of his becoming her boyfriend. And sometimes, that thought brought real regret.

Chapter Ten

As Abby watched the house turn into her salon, she felt as though she were living a dream.

Dreams were an important element in Hawaiian culture, and Abby had heard a lot about them from her father. A dream had been responsible for his moving his family to the mainland many years ago. He'd lost his job, and his brother in California had urged him to come; jobs were available there. But it was the dream her father had, of the three of them living in a small house, happy and healthy, that decided it.

And it had been the right decision, Abby knew, even though she'd regretted the move and decided to come back. It was a series of dreams that was responsible for that too.

The dreams started right after her breakup with

Jack. In them, she saw the house in Malino, the house where she'd lived until the age of twelve. Then old acquaintances began to people the dream. Aunty Lili. Julie. School friends. Even Kevin—a teenage Kevin. The dream recurred with increasing frequency. In her dreams, she'd cut the hair of the various people she saw.

Finally she decided that the dream was foretelling her destiny. She was meant to return to Malino, she just knew it. Luckily, she had the best parents in the world. When she finally told them about the dreams, and let them know that she really would like to return there to start a business, they were supportive. They agreed to back her in her new enterprise. They consulted Aunty Lili to inquire about jobs or business opportunities for Abby. And here she was. Her dream was almost reality.

The next few days passed in a blur. Excitement, anticipation, and fear warred within her. The Hair Place would open officially the following weekend, and Abby was anxious to have everything perfect. She wanted to move in, but because of Aunty Lili's worries, she decided to wait until Thursday. Her first official day of business would be Friday. She was delighted to have three scheduled appointments that day—Aunty Joy, who was one of Aunty Lili's friends, and the two daughters of Kevin's neighbor. She'd called to thank him for the floor tiles and to ask if he'd like to schedule his daughters on her opening day. She was tickled when he assured her that they would love being among the first to make use of The Hair Place. Abby told him to be sure and come in to see how nice the floor looked.

In the bustle of activity and packing, Abby found time to redo her own hair for the opening. She dispensed with her purple streaks, the object of so many remarks from Kevin, and so many strange looks from the more conservative islanders. Instead, she gave herself golden highlights, just the shade of her new walls. She liked the idea of matching her new salon, and Aunty Lili proclaimed herself relieved by her "normal" look.

To her surprise, Kevin claimed to miss the purple.

"What happened to your hair?" he asked, when she ran into the firefighters shopping for dinner supplies at the grocery store. "Where's the purple?"

Taken aback by his reaction, all Abby could think to say was, "Don't you like it?" She'd assumed that he, like most of the people in Malino, would prefer the golden color.

Jim and Dave both swore she looked gorgeous, but Kevin stared for a moment, considering.

"I miss the purple. It was you."

Abby pushed her cart away, shaking her head. Men!

On Wednesday night Abby busied herself packing her clothes, an anxious Mano following her every step. He could always tell when something different was going down, and he was not always happy about change. She was just offering him a few comforting pats when she received a frantic call from Julie.

"Abby, you've got to help me."

Julie used her best melodramatic voice, but Abby still felt her stomach clench. "What's wrong? You know I'll do what I can."

"It's my cousin. She's having this big sweet sixteen party and it's tomorrow, and I forgot all about it."

Julie's voice was in the upper register now, almost painful to Abby's ear. Still, Abby let out a breath of relief, unaware until then that she hadn't inhaled since Julie's first frenzied plea. At least there hadn't been a death, or an accident, or some kind of medical emergency. It was only life and death to Julie, who was still in full-fledged panic mode.

"I need a gift. You have to help me find something."

"You want to go shopping for a birthday gift?" Abby gave a short bark of laughter that was more relief than mirth. "Sure, I'll go shopping with you. I thought it was something really serious."

"This is serious," Julie insisted. "I can't show my face in the family if I don't get her something nice. She and I have always been close."

"Ooo-kay." Abby took a deep breath as she adjusted to Julie's histrionics. "When shall we go?"

"I'll pick you up in ten minutes. Are you at home or at the salon?"

"I'm at Aunty Lili's." She lowered herself onto the

bed, beside the suitcase she'd almost filled with her clothing. "I've been packing. Tomorrow is move-in day, you know."

"That's right. Oh, I'm sorry to pull you away tonight. But I *really* need help."

"That's okay. You know what Aunty keeps saying . . . 'Here in Hawaii, everybody help everybody.' "

They both laughed, Julie said she'd be right over, and they hung up. But not before Julie warned her to wear something nice enough for a good store.

Abby laughed as she glanced down at her clothes.

"What do you think, Mano," she asked the little dog who had become her constant companion, "are these shorts too grungy for Julie's sensibilities?"

She brushed at a paint smudge that appeared to be permanent, and decided that she did indeed need to change. Sighing at the extra effort required, she pulled a sundress from the suitcase. Still, Julie was always there for her. The least she could do was help out with something her friend saw as an emergency.

When Abby climbed into Julie's car some fifteen minutes later, she was still shaking her head— metaphorically—at Julie's melodramatic request.

"So, where are we going?"

Julie gave a huge, almost comic sigh. "I hate to have to drive all the way there, but I think we'll have to go to Kona to find something decent."

"Good thing I changed," Abby said. "Do you know what you're looking for? I thought you said you needed suggestions? I've been thinking hard ever since you called."

"Oh, yeah? What did you come up with?"

"I was thinking of clothes. A natural thought, since I was changing at the time," she added. "But the girls on the mainland are all wearing these cute flirty little skirts. It would be a nice gift."

"You think we could find something like that here?" The island was notoriously behind-times when it came to fashion items.

Abby shrugged. "I don't know. But there must be somewhere we can look. Maybe one of the hotel boutiques. That way we don't have to drive all the way into Kona either."

"Good idea. I just hope I can afford it." She threw a quick glance at the space between their seats, where she'd stashed her purse. "Oh, no!"

Julie's sudden exclamation drew Abby's attention. Now what?

"I don't have my credit card. I just realized . . . I still have the purse I take with me to work. See, it's a small one, because I don't carry a lot of stuff with me when I'm going to work. And I don't like to take my credit card and leave it around. You can't be too careful nowadays."

Abby had to agree with her on that.

"I don't know how I could have forgotten to change purses."

Julie's voice was heading into the upper registers once again. Abby thought she sounded almost as flustered as she had during her initial phone call.

"I guess I was so upset about not having a gift that I just grabbed this purse and left. We'll have to go back to my place."

"Don't worry about it." Abby didn't see the problem. "You can put it on my credit card and pay me back later."

"I can't let you do that." Julie's protest was earnest. "You have all these business expenses right now. You don't want to have anything extra adding to your limit."

"I guess not." It *was* nice of Julie to think of it, Abby decided, and she was losing the evening anyway. So it probably wouldn't matter if they took an extra fifteen minutes backtracking. Still, she was twitching at the delay, because she had so much to do before morning.

"I should have brought my nail polish," she said, as they stopped in front of Julie's house. "I could have done my nails while we drive down." She held her hands out in front of her. The salmon color she had on, decorated with tiny yellow flowers, had looked terrific with the halter top she'd donned in the morning. It was okay with the sundress, but she would have liked to have more of a coral shade.

"I'll hurry," Julie promised. "Don't worry, you'll get back in plenty of time to finish packing." She stuck her head back in the window. "You're so good to do this for me, Abby. Thanks."

Abby smiled. "Hey, you helped me with the salon, remember?"

As they drove past The Hair Place, Abby couldn't resist a quick glance. Anytime she drove by, she had to slow down so that she could admire her salon. She was so proud of the work she'd done. Except for the sign, the outside didn't look too different—that would have to wait. But the important inside was ready for her future clients.

"Wait a minute!"

Abby's sudden cry had Julie pressing her foot on the brake.

"What? What?"

Abby was twisting in her seat, pushing at the seat belt as it locked into place, preventing her from turning any further.

"There's a light on in the salon." Abby's voice was anxious, and her chest filled with dread. "I *know* I turned them all off. I'm very careful with the lights. You know how my dad is about not wasting energy."

"Should we stop?"

"Of course we should stop!" Abby almost shouted. "Maybe we should call 911." She reached for her cell phone while Julie entered the Dairy Queen parking lot to turn around.

"Do you think we should? What if it's nothing?"

Julie seemed concerned about a false alarm, and her nervousness was transferring to Abby.

"Maybe you could call my cousin Lono," Julie suggested.

Abby knew Lono was a local cop. That was okay by her. She knew that even if he wasn't currently on duty, he had the authority to make an arrest if there was a problem.

"What's his number?"

She dialed it, then handed the phone to Julie. "You'd better talk to him."

By then they were parked in front of The Hair Place. Abby was anxious to get out of the car and see what was going on. But she waited until Julie was done, her whole body twitching at the delay.

"He'll be right over," Julie said, handing the phone back to Abby. "We should probably wait out here."

"Are you nuts? I will go bananas if I have to wait out here. Come on." She opened the door of the car and stepped outside. "I can't believe anyone would still be in there, with the light on. I'm just worried that someone ripped me off. And just before I open too!" she almost wailed. "I haven't put my computer in yet, thank goodness, because I'm just using my laptop. But they could have taken my blowdryers and curling irons. My expensive scissors."

The more she thought about it, the more worried Abby became. Was she catching the worry bug from Aunty Lili?

Not sure whether to run up the steps—her first inclination—or proceed cautiously, Abby adopted an approach midway between the two. She walked slowly up the stairs, peering through the windows for anything she could see that didn't seem right. She felt like one of those amateur sleuths on television, sneaking up on some neighbor's house. All she needed was some brooding music to presage something terrible happening.

Those things don't happen in real life, Abby told herself. But this was her place, and she was emotionally involved. She could barely focus, and all she could see inside was the furniture and shadows.

She did, however have her key out well before they reached the door—and found it unlocked.

"Oh, no," she moaned. "Someone must have broken in." She stopped long enough to examine the door and frame. "At least the door isn't ruined. And the lock doesn't seem to be broken. They must have picked it."

She stepped inside, just as Lono's car pulled into the parking area. Julie stayed on the step to meet him.

With half her attention behind her on the approaching police officer, Abby was stunned when she heard the shout from a dozen voices.

"Surprise!"

Her eyes widened, and she thought she must have jumped a foot into the air. Her hands shaking with emotion, she blinked at the people who suddenly crowded the three openings to the inside room.

"Surprise!" they called out again. Laughter rang out as she continued to stand there, still trying to shift her mind from apparent robbery to surprise party.

Aunty Lili stepped forward, a plumeria lei in her hands. "You surprised, yeah?"

"I think we really caught her good," Mabel Akaka said, putting a second plumeria lei around her neck and cackling with delight.

"It wasn't easy hiding everybody inside that room—with all these new openings," Aunty Lili said.

"But it was more fun than my birthday party," Mrs. Akaka declared.

Abby was still standing just inside the door, stunned by the people milling around her. She'd suspected that Aunty and Julie might have a party for her opening, but she sure hadn't expected it tonight. Tomorrow, or even the next day, she might have been suspicious of Julie's sudden need for a shopping companion.

She turned to Julie, who'd stepped inside once the surprise was announced. "So you didn't need to shop for your cousin? It's not her birthday tomorrow?"

Julie laughed, along with Aunty and all the others close enough to hear what Abby asked.

"Oh, it's her birthday tomorrow," Julie said. "And I *would* be in big trouble if I didn't get her something nice, just like I said. What I didn't say is that I already got something. Last week. Sorry." She grinned. "And I had to pretend I forgot my credit card so Aunty Lili would have time to get over here."

They hugged, and Abby could feel the love and friendship that had gone into making this event happen. The scent of the plumerias drifted up to her nostrils, bringing back wonderful memories of celebrations earlier in her life.

As she and Julie parted, Abby noticed Lono standing in the doorway. In uniform. He was on duty this evening. "Oh, my gosh, are we in trouble for filing a false police report?"

"Yeah. You under arrest, Sistah."

Julie slapped him across his upper arm with the backside of her hand. "Lono. Shame on you. He was in on it too, Abby. Just in case you insisted on calling the police, which you did. I didn't want you to call 911."

"And there's another surprise," Aunty announced. "Come right in here."

She led Abby into the inner room, the lovely client waiting area she was so proud of. A sign hanging across the wall opposite the door proclaimed "Good Luck Abby," and crepe paper streamers in bright rainbow colors hung from the ceiling. A huge flower arrangement with a ribbon saying "Congratulations" sat on top of the television console.

But once Abby saw the couch, she had eyes for only that one small area of the room. Seated on her brightly-covered sofa was her mother.

Gabrielle rose, a wide smile on her face. "Surprise."

Abby walked straight into her mother's arms and rested her head on her shoulder. It felt wonderful to hug her, and she found herself close to tears. Tears of joy, of course. It had been less than a month, and she felt like a child for admitting it, but she'd missed her mother. She wanted to share this new phase of her life with her. How special that she was able to be here.

After a good long hug, she looked up and around, searching for another familiar face. Her mother whispered, "Daddy couldn't get away . . . but he sends his love."

Gabrielle finally pushed herself back, draping an orchid lei around her daughter's neck. "This place is beautiful. Everyone will love it. I'm so proud to be your mother. You're going to be a fine businesswoman."

As she stepped away from her mother, Abby realized there was someone else sitting on the sofa. Someone she hadn't even seen once Gabrielle's petite figure filled her visual field.

"Oh, my gosh. It's Patty, isn't it?" Abby approached the older woman sitting at the end of the couch—a small woman wearing a pink muumuu. One arm lay unmoving in her lap, and Abby suspected it had been permanently affected by her stroke. She gave her a hug, being careful not to jolt her. She was a tiny woman, and looked fragile. "I can't believe you're here. What do you think?" Abby gestured to the room at large.

Patty smiled, giving Abby's hand a gentle squeeze. "It's wonderful what you did with my old place. This is good, what you do here. You will have good business. Just like I did. Many happy years."

Impulsively, Abby removed one of her plumeria leis and put it around Patty's neck. She gave her another hug as she kissed her cheek.

"Thank you. I'll be building on what you started. Most of what we did here was cosmetic—you know, redecorating-type stuff."

While her friends discounted her attempt at downplaying what she'd accomplished, Abby looked around at everyone and felt a tear tremble on her lower eyelid. Besides the people she'd already noticed, the other ladies from the Hale Maika'i were there, beaming with joy at the special outing. Rebecca and Ramona stood beside the television with Marian and another young woman who must have been Kevin's older sister. The family resemblance was unmistakable. And at the back were not only Kevin, but Gil and Leila, and Greg and a young woman she recognized from the bank, his new wife.

Rounding out the group were Julie's parents and some of Aunty Lili's friends whom Abby had met at the house during the time she'd been staying there.

Abby blinked rapidly to halt the progress of any tears that might be considering overflowing onto her cheeks. "I'm so happy." Her voice broke on the last word, but she didn't cry.

"Hey, come on now, enough of this emotional stuff."

Abby had to smile. Leave it to Kevin to bring her back to earth.

"There's lots of food in the kitchen," Aunty Lili announced. "Everyone, go eat. Abby, you and your mom start off."

Still distracted, and emotionally drained, Abby nodded her acquiescence and led the way inside. It didn't feel right going ahead of so many senior citizens, but she'd been directed to do so by one of those very seniors.

Her perceptive mother gave her shoulder a squeeze. "Don't worry, honey. You're the guest of honor. Of course you should lead the food line."

Abby took a plate and glanced at Gabrielle as she helped herself to a piece of fried chicken.

"Did you get to see everything?" Abby asked. But before her mother could answer, Abby stopped, a scoop of potato salad halfway to the paper plate in her hand.

"Oh no, wait. What about Patty? Should I make a

plate for her?" She'd seen a wheelchair stashed in the corner of the sitting room, and she suspected it belonged to her frail landlady.

"I've got it." The answer came from a middle-aged Japanese woman behind Gabrielle. She stepped forward. "I'm Linda Okuda, Patty's daughter. I'll get a plate for Mother."

"It's so nice to meet you." Abby put down the serving spoon so that she could shake Linda's hand. "I'm so grateful to your mother for letting me rent this place at such a reasonable rate."

"Hey, what's happening."

"Talk story aftah . . ."

Grumbles from the line had Abby apologizing and quickly grabbing up her plate once more. "Boy, you people can turn on a person real fast," Abby teased, hurrying to fill her plate.

"Just don't keep us from our food," Kevin said—to general laughter.

Gabrielle had proceeded on ahead, so Abby now hurried after her, an overflowing plate balanced carefully in still shaky hands. She didn't have much of an appetite at the moment, but she didn't want to insult anyone by not trying their contribution. She couldn't believe how many people were there; she felt very special.

To her surprise, Gil and Leila were waiting for her in the sitting room instead of standing in line.

"We just wanted to wish you well," Leila said, hugging Abby as soon as she put her plate down on the coffee table. "We can't stay."

"Yeah, she's already called her mother twice to check on the baby, and we've only been here fifteen minutes," Gil grumbled. But it was a good-natured grumble, and Abby could see the love in his eyes when he looked at his wife.

Abby thanked them, and offered Leila a free hair-styling as a baby gift. "You'll be getting lots of things for the baby," Abby said, "so this can be just for you. Come on a day when Gil is home to watch David."

"You're a sweetheart," Leila told her, just as Kevin appeared with a heaping plate, Julie right behind him.

"Here you go," Kevin said, handing the plates over to the new parents. "Take it with you."

Abby smiled her thanks to her friends for thinking of it.

"Enjoy," she encouraged, walking Gil and Leila to the door.

By the time she returned to her neglected plate, everyone had found a place to sit, and a convivial atmosphere filled the room.

"Did you see the cards I brought from California?" Gabrielle asked her daughter.

"No." Abby looked around. "Oh, that basket? That's wonderful. I'll look at them after everyone leaves." She knew she would cry reading good luck messages from her friends and former colleagues in L.A., so she wanted to do that when she was alone.

"I told the women at Hale Maika'i about the party so that they could make cards," Julie told her. "Like your friends in L.A. did. But they wouldn't stop pestering me until I agreed to let them come," she finished with a laugh.

"I'm glad to see them. I got to attend a party there, so it's nice that they can come to one here."

Julie lowered her voice. "The dietician is going to have a fit when she hears what-all they're eating. But I'm not going to monitor diets tonight."

The women close enough to hear cheered.

As the guests settled down with their food, Kevin and Abby explained what had been done to renovate the salon. The compliments for the new décor came from every side and were completely sincere.

"When you go back into the kitchen, take a peek into the bedroom." Abby told everyone about the special gift from the Paleas. "I wasn't going to worry about painting that room until later."

"And they can all see Mano then too," Kevin said.

"Mano is here?"

Aunty Lili nodded. "I brought him over and put him in the bedroom with the gate up. We thought he might be upset with so many new people around. But he's been very good."

"So my wonderful watchdog has been here all along," Abby said. "And without a single warning bark to let me know what was happening."

There was general laughter and some quick comments about what a smart dog he was to keep the secret.

When everyone was finished with their food, someone lowered the lights and Aunty Lili carried in a sheet cake. Amid the scissors, hairdryers, and curlers decorating the top of the cake were the words, "Congratulations and good luck, Abby."

This time she couldn't prevent a tear or two dripping onto her cheeks. It was too much like her birthday party six weeks ago, when she'd made her secret wish. She'd wished for her new life to be perfect, for success in her business, and a lifetime of happiness. It was a lot to ask for—just for blowing out a few candles. Still, she figured she might as well think big. And look at what had happened. It might be too early to know for sure if all her wishes would come true, but things were well on their way.

And now she was getting a second chance. Someone provided three candles for the cake, saying three was a special number and asking her to blow it out "for business luck."

"Come on, honey," Aunty Lili said. "Take a deep breath and make a wish."

Abby closed her eyes. Making a wish was easy. This whole experience was part of her wish. She'd wished for a successful move to Malino. Now she wanted the rest of her dream. She wanted it all . . . a good life, a successful business, a man to love and marry. She wanted a man who loved her, a house and a family. She wanted *'ohana.*

A small smile tilted the corner of her lips. She opened her eyes and blew.

A cheer went up as all three candles were doused. *Really, what else could have happened,* she wondered, *with those three little candles?* But she was too happy to worry about the foolishness of such customs. And who was she to question whether or not it would bring her luck—she, who still believed in birthday wishes.

"You get your wish!" Julie shouted.

"Tell, tell."

"Don't be silly, she can't tell." Julie rounded on the person who'd asked Abby to reveal her wish—one of the women from the care center. Her tone was gently scolding. "You don't get your wish if you tell."

As Julie took over the cutting of the cake, with Mabel supervising, Abby turned to her mother.

"I still can't believe you're here." She clasped her mother's hand, as if still trying to accept that she was more than a dream vision.

"I found a great deal online. I'm only staying through Sunday," she said. "I wanted to be here to see you launch your new business. Your father would have liked to come too, but he couldn't get away right now. They're really short-handed since the last budget cuts."

Abby nodded. It was such a common story these days.

"I feel like I never left Malino," she said. "I can't wait for Daddy to retire so that you two can come back too."

The party began to break up soon after the cake was consumed. Julie had to get the Hale Maika'i women back to the center, and Patty's daughter seemed concerned that her mother might overdo it.

"We still have the long drive back to Kona," she told Abby as they said their good-byes.

Patty had tears in her eyes as she wished Abby all the best.

"I'm so happy to have you working here. I know it will be good," she said, finishing up with a firm nod of her head.

In the end, only Abby, Kevin, Aunty Lili, and Gabrielle remained. Anxious to give her mother a personal tour, Abby led them all through the house, telling her mother about the changes she and Kevin had wrought. At the bedroom door, Abby removed the gate, allowing Mano the freedom of the house. He didn't seem too upset about having been relegated to the one room; he didn't run through the house in delight at his freedom. He just wagged his tail, standing at Abby's feet, waiting patiently for one of them to pet him. Which, of course, they all did.

"I want you to see how pretty the bedroom turned

out," Abby said, leading her mother into the small room. To complement the wall color, Abby had put a blue bulb in the overhead light fixture. She had a brighter bulb in a bedside lamp, in case she wanted to read in bed. But the effect of the overhead light in the blue room made the onlookers gasp. As Abby had told her mother on the phone a week ago, it was like sitting at the bottom of the ocean.

"I'm going to get one of those CDs with ocean sounds to play in here," Abby announced. "Won't it be perfect?"

Behind her, Kevin examined the room with interest. He hadn't been in it since the day they'd painted. *You can tell a lot about a woman by the way she decorates her bedroom*, he thought. And Abby's was definitely a revelation. Not the stark, modern look he'd expected from the young woman with purple highlights and ten earrings. But then, contradictions were one of the things he most appreciated about Abby. For her bedroom, Abby had covered the windows with sheer white lace curtains, and put old-fashioned crocheted doilies on top of the antique vanity. A silver vanity set that looked quite old sat on one of the doilies. Her bed was covered with a frilly confection of a quilt, trimmed with lace and embroidery. It looked worn, and he wondered if she'd picked it up at a garage sale, or brought it with her from the mainland.

The question was quickly answered by Abby's exclamation of surprise.

"You brought my bedspread with you!" She turned to her mother with pleasure. "Thank you. I was going to ask you about sending it. Doesn't it go great in the room?"

A smile played at Kevin's lips as he thought this over. So this wasn't a new style for her. Her old bedroom must have been similar if the old quilt worked so well.

Kevin pondered her decorating choices, wondering what insight he might gain about Abby's personality from it all. It seemed likely that Abby had a more feminine side—a side she usually let show only by the way she did her fingernails. He'd often thought it an anomaly, the way she redid her nails every day so that they matched her clothing—even the old clothes she used for painting and other grub work. The athlete he saw in her didn't compute with a woman who painted little flowers on her nails to match her sundress, or decorated them with glittery little gems. Yep, contradiction could be Abby Andrews' middle name.

Abby was also pondering the bedroom's décor, though not because she was seeking insight into her decorative choices. She was staring because she realized that her things were lying on the dresser and vanity tops. Not just the things her mother must have brought, like the comforter and vanity set, but the things she'd been packing when Julie pulled her away from Aunty's house earlier. When she left, everything on the dresser here had still been on the dresser there.

She opened a drawer and found herself staring at her underwear, neatly sorted and folded into stacks. She rapidly pushed the drawer closed, noting that Kevin was further back in the room and probably— hopefully—hadn't seen into the drawer. A soft pink suffused her cheeks anyway. Underwear was such a personal thing.

"How did my things get here?"

"We brought them," Aunty replied with a grin. "Gabrielle arranged everything once I got it here. It wasn't so hard. But we had to hurry. We didn't know how long Julie could stall at her place."

"You're all moved in now," Aunty told her. "I know you've been wanting to be here, and you were humoring me by staying all this time."

Abby didn't know what to say.

"I'll be staying with you," Gabrielle said. "Nice that the place came with a sofa bed."

"Mom. I can't let you come all this way and then have to sleep on a sofa bed. You take the bedroom."

But Gabrielle insisted she'd be fine. "I can't take you away from this special room on your first night in the house. I'll be just fine. But it was nice of you to offer."

Once everyone was gone, Abby and her mother settled onto either end of the sofa, Mano curled up between them. They sat there into the wee hours, talking.

"I like your Kevin," Gabrielle said.

"Mom, he's not my Kevin."

Her mother ignored her, smiling gently instead. "I think he likes you."

"We're friends. We got to be friends while we were redoing the house."

"There's nothing wrong with being friends. Ask Aunty Lili sometime about Emma and Matt Correa. They were best friends for most of their lives. And your friend Greg was telling me about how he and Kim got together. They knew each other in high school, then they got to be friends again when he came back here to practice." Gabrielle nodded. "Friendship is a good way to begin."

"Well, whether or not anything more develops, I'm happier than I've been in years." The ends of her lips quirked upward, a testimony to her words.

"I can tell," her mother assured her. "And it makes me happy too." Gabrielle sobered. "I worried when you said you wanted to come here to start your own salon. Even though Aunty Lili told me she thought it was a good idea, that Malino could use its own salon.

It's tough starting a business. But now that I've seen what you've done, and seen the friends you already have here . . ." She broke off to give Abby a hug. "I think you're going to be just fine."

Chapter Eleven

Ten months later . . .

Abby could hardly believe it, but it was the night before her twenty-fourth birthday. One year ago, she was blowing out her candles at home in Santa Monica. Tomorrow, she'd be blowing out candles at her own home/business in Malino.

It had been an unbelievable year. She'd left California to start a new life in the town where she had spent her first twelve years. The little girl who'd hated to leave returned a woman who'd grown up in the modern city of Los Angeles, a woman who dressed in a modish style common in L.A. but unusual in a small town in rural Hawaii.

Blowing out her candles a year ago, she'd wished for a new start. And what better way than to move back to Hawaii, to the little town where she still had friends and relatives? Her birthday wish, at least the part about leading a fulfilling life and having success in her business venture, had been fulfilled. Malino had welcomed her with the warmest of alohas. While she wouldn't become rich running her salon, she was successful enough to pay her bills. And she felt sure business would continue to improve. She'd always heard that the first year was the hardest.

She and Kevin continued the friendship that had begun with their work together on the salon renovation. They both enjoyed athletic pursuits, and got together to jog in the park, to swim and fish, or just to sit and talk.

At first, it was hard for Abby to be around Kevin and not hope that things between them would advance in a more romantic direction. But one day she realized what could happen if they began to *really* date. They might find that they weren't as suited as she thought, and Kevin might tell her he was no longer interested in her friendship. She didn't want to take a chance on that. So she clung to their sweet relationship and tried hard not to want more.

Her new life was full to overflowing. She and Mano were regulars along Malino's beachfront park, where they greeted other joggers and walkers each day. She'd been asked to help with the annual Kamehameha Day pageant, and with the Christmas pageant. She'd started an exercise class—at first with just herself and Julie in the salon's sitting room. As they told others about it, the group grew until they had to use a room at the church to fit all the women who wanted to participate. Abby even found and attended a training program for aerobics instructors so that she could better direct the sessions.

Best of all, she had a large group of regular clients at The Hair Place. Just as she'd envisioned, the comfortable sitting room was often filled with women "talking story," that favorite of island pastimes. During the summer, the room became a place for Malino's teenage girls to hang out. Abby didn't mind them reading the style magazines she tried to keep on hand, and she loved the way they lavished attention on Mano. Her collection of old movies became a popular way to spend a rainy afternoon.

Hoping to appeal to more teens, Abby often turned on MTV when she had young clients. To her surprise, the music videos became popular with the older set, as well. Aunty Lili's friends were titillated by the costumes and dancing routines—often giggling in feigned outrage as they watched, spellbound. Abby hoped she wasn't corrupting Malino's senior citizens.

And now it was time for another birthday party. She'd told Aunty Lili and Julie in a firm voice that she'd have no surprises this year. Last year's dedication party had been surprise enough for years to come. She still felt flustered when she remembered

how she'd insisted on calling 911, and had just barely been deflected by Julie.

Aunty Lili insisted on organizing a party, but
promised to have it on the day after her birthday.

"Friday evening is okay," she told Abby, whose
birthday fell on a Friday. "But Saturday afternoon is
better for everybody. We'll have a potluck again, like
for the salon opening. Don't you worry, I'll take care
of everything."

Abby thought herself perfectly capable of handling
the arrangements, but deferred to Aunty Lili. She *was*
busy, and she knew Aunty would enjoy it.

"Tell them no gifts," she said.

Aunty Lili nodded, but Abby wondered. Aunty
Liliuokalani always had an agenda of her own.

"And you should take Friday off," Aunty Lili told
her. "It's your birthday, you can do something special."

"Like what?"

"Ask Kevin. He'll think of something." Aunty
smiled.

Ask Kevin? Somehow she couldn't quite bring herself to do it. But she wasn't terribly surprised when
he brought it up. *Had Aunty given him a little nudge?*
she wondered.

"I heard about your birthday party on Saturday,"
Kevin told her as they walked back toward the salon,
cooling down from a run along the beach. Abby had
left Mano at home; he was too small to keep up with
them when they did their running. She'd take him for

a stroll later. "Would you like to have dinner with me on Friday? I'll take you somewhere nice."

Abby couldn't help but laugh. "Somewhere nice? Sure. I'd love to."

"Are you working on Friday?"

"Probably not. Aunty Lili told me I should take the day off, and she must have spread the word. I haven't had any calls about appointments, though I wouldn't mind taking a few early in the day."

"Good." They were back at the salon, and Kevin opened the door for her. "Get your book. I want to make an appointment for Friday afternoon around one."

"What?"

Abby's one failure in the past year had been her inability to get Kevin into The Hair Place for a haircut. She didn't understand why he was so reluctant, but it was the one thing she could not talk him into. So now, when he suggested putting his name into her schedule, Abby feigned a fainting fit. She put the back of her hand to her forehead and reached out to the counter for support.

"Wait, wait. I must not have heard you correctly. Did you say you wanted to make an appointment? For a haircut?"

Kevin nodded. He knew Abby had been hurt that he hadn't come before now. But he was working at self-preservation with his adamant refusals. He enjoyed their friendship, and didn't want to complicate it.

A haircut might seem like a simple thing, but he wasn't sure he could handle it. She'd have to put her hands in his hair, massage his scalp. He knew she would be totally professional, but he wasn't sure he could be. Even *thinking* about her hands on him made his heart race. There was a chemistry between them that he'd noticed back when they were painting her salon. He was sure she'd been aware of it too. He didn't know how she coped with it, but his method was to ignore it and try not to get into situations where they had to be too close, or touch one another. He felt they had a good friendship based on shared interests and mutual respect. Why damage it?

Also, he admitted that he was a coward—a relationship coward. He didn't want to get involved with Abby, fall in love with her—something he thought might be a little too easy to do—and then have her decide to leave Malino. Kevin liked small-town life, and wanted to pass the experience on to his children when he had them. So he had to keep Abby's friendship long enough to see if Malino was right for her.

Who would have guessed that a woman who had lived in Los Angeles for her formative years could return to a small town and manage to fit in? She often said it was like she'd never left, and—finally—he believed her. In the year since she'd arrived, he hadn't seen any frustration on her part with the small-town mentality, or homesickness for things not available in the islands. She was perfectly happy to watch a video on a Saturday night, even though she talked about the Broadway shows she'd seen in Los Angeles, and the trendy clubs she'd visited. But she always spoke about L.A. in the past tense, much like people referred to their college years, looking back on them with nostalgia but not regret.

He offered a wry smile at her fainting act. "I decided it was time I follow the rest of Malino into The Hair Place."

"Great. I can't wait to get my scissors in your hair."

Her impish grin made his heart flip over. Oh, yes, it was time. She'd spent a year in Malino, getting involved in all aspects of life there. He'd spent a year getting to know all sides of the complex woman that was Abby. Now he had plans. And the first step was to get his hair cut.

"So, you lasted the year."

If Abby thought it was a strange way to begin their conversation, she didn't let on. It was Friday afternoon, Abby's twenty-fourth birthday, and Abby sat Kevin at the mirror so that she could explain what she wanted to do with his hair. "No surprises," she'd promised when she made the appointment for him.

"Of course." She dismissed his comment as if it was silly for anyone to question whether or not she would stay for that amount of time. "I told you when I arrived that I was going to stay forever."

So she had. But not everyone had believed her.

"A lot of people thought you'd miss the big city. But you fit right in," he said. "Do you ever miss Los Angeles?"

She met his eyes in the mirror, as serious as he was. "Sometimes I miss my parents. But I love it here. I've never regretted the move."

She put her fingers into his hair, fluffing it out away from his head.

"But on to business. I've been dying to cut your hair, you know. Ever since we first met."

"That long?" He couldn't help a quirk of the lips. "What's wrong with my hair?"

"Nothing. It's just not the best style for you, taking in the shape of your head and all." She grinned at his image in the mirror. "Take my word for it, Kevin, I'm a professional."

Abby could see the tension in his body, and she wondered if he just didn't like to get his hair cut. Some people did have a phobia about it, like going to the dentist. Rare, but possible. Maybe he trimmed it himself. The long length and lack of design made that a distinct possibility.

"You have really nice hair," she said, pushing her fingers through the thick strands and examining the texture. She noticed that he stiffened, and thought again about the possibility of a phobia.

"But your hair is very thick, and the cut isn't taking that into consideration. You have this heavy roll of hair here." She ran her fingers through his hair again, showing him what she meant.

Unfortunately, she was having trouble keeping her mind on the moment. His hair felt good. It was soft and clean, not at all dry. A clean, faintly citrusy scent drifted up to her nostrils, and she couldn't resist smoothing the strands between her fingers.

"Healthy hair, though. You're lucky there. You must take good care of it."

Kevin dismissed that comment by ignoring it. *Typical male,* she thought.

"It just sticks out like that because you pushed it all out with your fingers."

Abby almost laughed. "No. I may have pulled it out some, but it's the cut that's making it do that." She picked up a comb and applied it to his head, doing her best to arrange his hair neatly. To her professional eyes, it just did not look good even when it lay smooth and in place.

"You see, there's too much hair here." She ran her fingers around his head, indicating the area that needed help. "It changes the shape of your head. You have a nice oval face, but with all this hair here, it makes your head look wider in the middle. Top heavy."

She watched his reflection in the mirror, waiting until he met the eyes of her reflection. Then she gave him her best smile.

"But don't worry, I can fix it."

* * *

Kevin sat in the reclining chair in front of the shampoo basin and hoped Abby would get on with the haircut, and do it quickly. The touch of her small but strong hands on his head made him feel like a coiled spring. He'd wanted to pop up out of that chair and rush right out the door and back to the small house he'd purchased just a year before her arrival. He was proud to have his own place. It was near enough to the home he'd grown up in that he could keep in close touch with his mother, and help her out when necessary. Yet it was all his. He valued his private time there. With a job that involved so much group activity, his home was truly his castle.

Lately, however, he found thoughts of Abby intruding on his privacy. He'd always cherished his leisure time, using it to revitalize himself by listening to music and working on his own property. The house had needed a lot of work, and he'd been doing it slowly. He'd started out in his bedroom, deciding that that well-used room was the most important. After that, he'd tackled the kitchen. Two rooms in a year didn't seem like much, but he'd had other things happening as well. Abby wasn't the only one he'd helped with remodeling tasks.

"See, now, isn't this nice? Aren't you sorry you waited so long to come in?"

Abby was shampooing his hair, and he had to admit it felt good. *Waaay* too good. Her strong fingers massaged his scalp, getting the blood circulating. He didn't know how she managed to keep her nails from interfering.

"It's okay," he finally said.

Actually, it was more than okay. A languid feeling, beginning in his well-massaged scalp, spread down into his chest and out into his arms, making his fingers tingle. He wanted to close his eyes and dream about Abby, not get up and walk back to the other room.

Abby finished rinsing off his hair and put a towel over it to absorb the excess water.

"Come on. Let's get you into the chair."

"Funny, I thought I was sitting in a chair."

"Oh, you're a riot."

But she did smile at him. Kevin drank it in, noting the presence of that cute dimple. Then he saw what she held in her hands.

"Good grief, you're not going to use that, are you?"

Abby looked down at the cape she held, bright orange with streaks of other colors scattered across it like confetti.

"Oops, sorry. It's my favorite one because it's so bright and cheerful. And the women like it. But I have a dull black one for the men," she added, shoving the orange cape into a drawer and pulling out a plain black one. She draped it around his shoulders, then began to comb his hair.

Kevin found the experience interesting. He'd never

had a woman cut his hair before. Not that he was a chauvinist, it was just that he'd been going to the same barbershop since he was a boy. Mr. Ando, who cut men's hair from a tiny shop right near the fire station, already seemed ancient when Kevin was a boy, but he'd kept on with his work until a few years ago. When he retired, his son took over, and all his customers continued on without even a blip in their routines.

This was definitely different. Abby combed his hair carefully, checking it from all angles. Then she began trimming, one small section at a time—with scissors. No noisy electric clippers for her.

"Where are we going for dinner?"

Her question caught him unawares. He was still trying not to notice how much he liked the way she touched him as she worked on developing his hairstyle.

"It's a surprise."

She met his eyes in the mirror, pouting at him for not telling.

"I'm not sure I like surprises."

"No kidding?" Kevin asked. "You know, Abby, I think you might be a control freak. You always want to know what's going on."

"No, it's just that you all gave me such a scare last year . . ."

Kevin just stared.

"Well, okay." She stopped cutting for a moment,

meeting his eyes again in the mirror. "Maybe I do like to know what's happening. Nothing wrong with that."

Amusement lit Kevin's eyes. Even after a whole year in his company, she was still awed by the sight of those clear blue eyes. No one else in his family had eyes like his, though she supposed that his grandfather Charles must have.

She turned back to his haircut. He was going to look so good! She did have to step back metaphorically, however. Working so intimately with his hair was much too appealing. Once again she reminded herself that she had to protect her heart. It was too late to stop herself from falling in love. Last summer, she'd admitted to herself—and she might have shared the secret with Mano—that she'd fallen in love with Kevin. But in order to hold on to their special friendship, she'd determined that she could not let him know. Julie had told her how he'd been hurt many years ago by a woman who left him for a different lifestyle on the mainland. She knew that made him leery. As long as she continued to spend time with him, Abby didn't mind that their relationship was platonic.

Finally, she stepped back from the chair. "There you are. What do you think?"

Kevin had stopped watching her work, just enjoying the feel of having her touch his hair. With his eyes closed, he could relax and daydream about her running her fingers through it for reasons other than

styling. And his dream hadn't stopped with his hair.
Her small hands were moving across his chest, mas-
saging his shoulders . . .

"What?"

His startled return to consciousness made Abby
laugh.

"What happened, did you fall asleep? I have to tell
you, that's a first for me." She gestured to the mirror.
"I'm done. What do you think?"

Kevin looked at his reflection. He blinked and
looked again.

"That's amazing."

Amazing? Had he said amazing? Kevin was glad
no one else was in the salon. But he was fairly
stunned by the sight of his own reflection. Abby had
been correct. His face looked completely different
now that she'd "shaped" his hair.

"Good grief, I look like one of those guys on that
'Queer Eye' show."

"Is that good?"

"I don't know." He liked it, he decided. But he was
going to have to put up with a lot of kidding from the
guys.

"I'm going to take that as a compliment."

She pulled the cape from around him and brushed
at his shoulders with her hands. Kevin had to take a
deep breath to keep from swatting her away. She
wouldn't understand how her mere touch made him
crazy. He'd finally admitted that he loved Abby—

Abby with her strange hair and row of earrings, though she had tempered her hairstyle over the past year, letting it grow out a bit and using quieter colors for her streaks. Well, except for the bright red at Christmas. And the green for St. Patrick's Day. And . . .

"So what time shall I be ready?"

Kevin almost didn't know what she was talking about. Her presence so distracted him, he could barely keep his mind on their conversation. But, of course, she was referring to dinner.

"Ah, how about six?"

Abby wanted to look special for her date with Kevin. Not that it was an official date, but he had asked her out to dinner. So it qualified as a date in her mind.

She sat at the vanity table in what she called her "underwater room" and checked her makeup yet again. She didn't want to use a lot, but she wanted to look her very best. Beside her, Mano sat watching.

"I know, I know. I'm being ridiculous."

She took a square of cotton and wiped off the eye shadow she'd just applied.

"Too much, huh? I'll just use a touch of the brown."

She brushed on the new color, frowning at her reflection. But before she could do anything more, there was a knock at the back door.

Abby stood, smoothing down her dress. She'd chosen one of the few good dresses she owned, a designer dress she'd gotten at a thrift shop in L.A. Because of the unique cut, it draped over her body like a second skin, and she'd always felt that the deep forest green color was very complimentary.

"Okay, Mano. This is it. I guess I'm ready."

She picked up her small handbag and headed for the kitchen.

Kevin could only stare when Abby opened the door. He'd told her they'd go somewhere special, but he still couldn't believe how great she looked. Her dress was like something a movie star would wear, and she'd twisted her hair together somehow so that it looked like she wore a natural headband of her own hair.

"Wow."

His impromptu compliment made Abby smile.

"Thanks."

He wondered if she felt as awkward as he did. They'd been great friends for a year, but most of their time together was spent in various athletic activities. This was completely different. This was a date, with a capital D. Except that it wasn't.

Suddenly, Kevin felt guilty. But he'd planned the evening carefully, and he couldn't back out now. Too many others were involved. He'd have to make it up to Abby some other time.

"Well, shall we go? Do you have a sweater or something?"

She had something—a fuzzy, lacy thing that draped over her shoulders and made him want to hug her close.

Kevin escorted her to his car, opening the door for her. He noticed that she didn't object this evening.

Abby settled her skirt around her carefully, not wanting to arrive with too many wrinkles. She wondered where they were going, and whether Kevin would tell her if she asked now. Might as well try.

"So, where to?"

Kevin didn't take the bait. "You'll see."

But when he pulled up a short time later, Abby was sure there must be some mistake. They were in the parking lot of the high school.

"We're at the school." She felt dumb saying it, but they couldn't be eating dinner there. She must have missed something, daydreaming about Kevin falling in love with her.

"Yes," Kevin confirmed. "Ramona called just before I got to your place. She apologized profusely, but asked if I could pick up a book she thinks she left in the cafeteria. She needs it tomorrow, and Ma is out with the car, so she couldn't get back for it."

He opened the car door, but didn't get out immediately. "I'll only be a minute. Want to come with me?"

Abby looked at his lean, muscular figure, hesitating on the edge of the car seat. He looked terrific—

toned and tanned, and wearing a blue Aloha shirt with a pair of dark trousers. For Hawaii, it was a dressy outfit.

"Sure. Why not?"

She might as well walk with him. If she stayed in the car, she'd just have more time to dream. She'd done too much of that already. It was better to approach their friendship in a more realistic manner.

Abby climbed out of the car, completely forgetting to wait for Kevin to come around and open her door. After all, pals didn't use that kind of courtesy with each other. But Kevin hurried around, grabbing the open door and waiting for her, then closing it behind her.

They walked toward the cafeteria together.

"Will it be open?" Abby asked.

"Sure. They clean after school, and it takes time. And they often have meetings or games."

He put his arm around Abby's waist, his hand resting lightly on the small of her back. Heaven help her, but it felt so nice, her knees actually buckled and she stumbled. Which meant Kevin reached out and put his arms around her. He didn't just support her, he pulled her against him, holding her within his arms like a precious object. Abby felt ready to collapse, to become just a puddle of human gel on the ground outside the high school cafeteria.

"Are you okay?" Kevin asked.

He continued to hold her, much too close for her

comfort. Her heart thumped so heavily in her chest, she thought that he must surely hear it. His eyes looked down into her face and she felt as though he was peering into her soul. She could see her reflection in his eyes, and it seemed to be growing larger. He was lowering his head. He was going to kiss her!

Abby knew she needed some air, but it was impossible for her to take more than a shallow breath. Her eyelids lowered. Her lips parted.

It had been almost a year since their last kiss. Abby had wonderful memories of that kiss, memories so glorious, she knew she must have exaggerated her remembrance of it. Now she learned that she had not. Kevin's lips were soft and warm, gentle against hers. His breath tasted of mint and for one horrible moment she wondered if she would explode into giggles, imagining him on her doorstep making use of a breathmint or spray.

Then he increased the pressure of his lips against hers, and any urge to giggle evaporated. Her arms reached up around him, her fingers trailed up into his newly cut hair. She hadn't cut it too short, hoping for just this chance. She loved running her fingers through his hair, and took the opportunity to bury her hands in its wavy strands.

It seemed like a minute. It seemed like an hour. When Kevin broke off the kiss, Abby stood unmoving, too numb to say or do anything.

Kevin placed another quick kiss on her lips and

turned her toward the door of the cafeteria, his arm still around her waist.

"I guess we'd better find that book."

The book. That's right. Ramona's book. Abby's brain was so muddled, she barely remembered where they were. She just wanted to get on with dinner so they could get to the good-night part. She hoped he'd kiss her again. He'd *better* kiss her again. They couldn't leave it like this. He appeared to be taking their relationship to a new level, and she couldn't wait.

Kevin stepped forward, but didn't allow her to fall behind. His arm remained firmly planted at her waist as he pulled open the cafeteria door.

Chapter Twelve

"**S**urprise!"

Abby jumped about a foot, grabbing onto Kevin's arm to prevent herself falling. *Surprise* was right! What the heck was going on here?

The cafeteria was filled with people. Familiar people. They'd done it to her again!

Aunty Lili materialized beside her, an orchid lei in her hands. She draped it over Abby's head, kissing her cheek. "Happy birthday, Abby. Surprise."

Abby hugged her aunt, shocked at the giggle that escaped from the older woman's lips.

"What's going on?"

"We had so much fun at the party we gave you last year. We decided we had to have another one," Aunty Liliuokalani said.

"Besides," Julie said, popping up beside Aunty Lili, and putting a ti leaf lei around Abby's neck, "you were so determined not to let us surprise you with another party."

"Yep," Kevin agreed. "How could we resist a challenge like that?"

Now Abby was really confused. So what about the kiss? Was he just trying to distract her, so she didn't suspect the cafeteria was filled with her friends? Or was it as spontaneous as it seemed? And most important of all, did he actually mean it?

There was no time to think of that now. Abby looked around at the faces of her friends. She couldn't be angry with any of them. Everyone was so happy at catching her out for a second time. Next year, she vowed, she'd pay more attention.

The party was a complete success. Everyone had a good time, from the women of the Hale Maika'i care center to little eleven-month old David Rezentes. But Abby thought she might have had the most fun of all.

"Speech, speech."

Abby glared at Julie. "I don't want to make a speech," she said. "What would I say?"

"Just tell everyone how much you've enjoyed the past year," her friend urged.

So Abby got up and talked about her year in Malino.

"I hardly know what to say. It's been an awesome

year. I left here at twelve, and came back last year at twenty-three. With crazy hair and rows of earrings and a box of old videos. And maybe you didn't know this, but with a broken heart. And you all accepted me back, making me feel like I never left at all. And now my heart is mended, my business is a success, and I count all of you as my friends. My family—my *'ohana.* Last year when I blew out the candles on my birthday cake, I made a secret wish—a birthday wish. I wanted a new start, success in starting my own business, and personal happiness. I think all my wishes came true. Thanks to the people of Malino." She swallowed hard, hoping she wouldn't cry. *"Mahalo nui loa."*

Her thank-you-very-much was swallowed up by the thunderous applause. Someone at the back of the room started strumming on a guitar. This was soon joined by a ukulele, and then by several voices raised in song. Her party would be going on for some time. Everyone was having too much fun to go home in the near future.

"At least you told them not to bring gifts." Abby put her arm around Aunty Lili and squeezed. "You're the best, Aunty Lili."

"I told them no gifts, but not everybody listened."

Abby looked puzzled. "I didn't see any gifts."

Aunty Lili looked wise, but didn't say more. Kevin came up behind Abby, putting his arms around her and pulling her to one side.

"Hey, birthday girl."

"Hey, yourself. I guess you, Aunty Lili, and Julie planned all this, huh?"

His answer was an enigmatic smile. "Let's just say all your friends got together."

Abby put her arms around him, enjoying the close contact. He didn't seem to mind that they stood together, hugging, in the presence of most of the town.

"Let's step outside. I have something for you."

She frowned. "I thought I said no gifts."

"That was for the general admission. I'm special."

Abby had to laugh. "Think you're so clever, don't you?"

Kevin just smiled, leading her outside. Back where they'd shared that wonderful kiss. Could it be that he wanted another? Abby's vision blurred as she remembered that exquisite moment, and hoped for an encore.

Kevin led her to a spot beside the building where a jacaranda tree grew from the green lawn. The night was cool, the air rife with the earthy scent of plants and newly mowed grass. The security lights lent a full-moon glow to the lawn, and created dappled patterns on the grass beneath their feet that shifted with the rhythm of the trade winds.

Kevin took her into his arms and kissed her again. Abby held on tight, not just because she loved the feel of his solid strength, but because she was afraid she'd fall flat on her face if she didn't have his support. His kisses got better and better, and she couldn't believe how much she wanted him to continue. She wondered how long they could stay out there before someone came looking for them.

As Kevin raised his head, she found herself giggling. It was just too funny—two people their age making out under a tree on the high school lawn. She shared this thought with Kevin, and was happy to hear his laughter added to hers.

"That's not why I brought you out here. I just couldn't resist stealing a kiss first."

Abby, for once at a loss for words, just stared into his eyes.

"I guess you're wondering what this all means."

"Definitely. Not that I'm objecting," she added. "You're a great kisser, Kevin." Her eyes twinkled as she relived the moment.

But Kevin didn't allow her to remain in the past.

"I wanted to tell you how happy I am that you moved back to Malino. And that Aunty Lili asked me to help you with the renovations at the salon. Your friendship has been very important to me this past year, Abby." He looked into her face, as though trying to read her mind. "Has it been the same for you?"

"Oh, yes." Abby clasped his hands to her. "Our friendship is one of the best things about the past year. Everything has been wonderful, but I don't know if I would have been nearly so happy if I didn't have you to do things with."

"I was afraid you wouldn't like it here. That you'd be bored."

"I know a lot of people thought I would go back to California. But I thought you knew me better than that, Kevin."

"I was afraid," he admitted. "It's why I didn't let you cut my hair, you know."

"You have a phobia about getting your hair cut?"

"What?"

Kevin was so shocked, Abby knew she'd gotten *that* wrong.

"I thought you had some kind of phobia about having someone cut your hair. I thought you must trim it yourself."

Kevin laughed—full, deep-bodied laughter that shook his whole frame. Finally, he wiped his eyes and looked at Abby.

"I didn't let you cut my hair because having your hands on me made me crazy."

Abby felt a thrill at his words.

"Crazy? Really?"

"Really." He swallowed. "Abby, I think I love you."

"Sounds like a song." Immediately, Abby regretted saying it. But she couldn't think when she was as flustered as Kevin made her. He was too close. She just hoped he wasn't mad. That he didn't think she was being flippant at such an important moment.

Kevin frowned, and Abby held her breath.

"You see what you do to me? You've got me talking in song lyrics."

Abby smiled. "Next you'll be singing Broadway show tunes."

"I hope not," he said with a shudder, while Abby's smile segued into a chuckle.

Kevin took her hands in his and inhaled deeply. He looked into her eyes, and her smile disappeared.

"Abby, I think you and I could have a good life together here in Malino. Will you marry me?"

Abby shouted, leaping into the air and clutching him around the neck, her feet dangling a foot off the ground. Kevin almost went down, but managed to recover his balance and hold them both upright.

"Was that a yes?" His eyes remained focused on her face.

She grinned, dropping a kiss on his forehead. "That was a *yes!*"

"I was hoping you'd say that."

Kevin put her down, reaching into his pocket and bringing out a ring. "I hope you like it," he said, slipping it onto the third finger of her left hand. "If not, we'll go together to choose something else."

Not a conventional ring for his unconventional woman, Abby thought. She stared down at a beautiful emerald-cut blue topaz. It was the blue of Kevin's eyes, the blue of the Pacific Ocean.

"It's perfect, Kevin. Absolutely perfect. I love it."

"Let's go tell the world."

Pulling her by the hand, he led the way back to the cafeteria.

"I wish my parents were here."

"We'll call them as soon as the party's over."

"Kevin." Abby stopped, planting her feet firmly three feet from the door. She waited until he turned to face her before she spoke. "I love you."

His eyes filled with tenderness. "I love you too."

"Good." Abby's arms slipped around his neck. "Kiss me again."

When Aunty Lili peeked out, she saw Kevin and Abby locked in each other's arms. She also noted a flash of blue light that came from the third finger of Abby's left hand.

With a smile as wide as the ocean, Aunty Liliuokalani pulled her head in and closed the door.